Sanity by Sunrise

Sanity by Sunrise

A NIGHT OF
POST-TEACHING STRESS
SYNDROME

Diana!
This book healed
me in my guilt + suffering
after teaching!
Enjoy.

Gary Weibye

Gary O. Weibye

Library of Congress Number: 00-192691
ISBN #: Hardcover 1-4010-5052-2
Softcover 0-7388-4689-9

This is a work of fiction. Names, characters, places and incidents either are the product of the author's imagination or are used fictitiously, and any resemblance to any actual persons, living or dead, events, or locales is entirely coincidental.

This book was printed in the United States of America.

To order additional copies of this book, contact:
Xlibris Corporation
1-888-7-XLIBRIS
www.Xlibris.com
Orders@Xlibris.com

Contents

TO EVERYONE WHO EVER PICKED UP A PIECE OF
CHALK AND STEPPED OUT THERE,
INCLUDING MY SON.

-WEIB

Chapter One

This is the way it happens.

You burn out, and you quit going to work. You fill out a pile of papers, and you walk out of there. You find a way to get to your idyllic mountain top, and the thing's done. Then one night, very late, as you are up again fogging around your living room, you catch sight of your undead self in a reflection off some glass surface, and you say, "My God. This could go on for another twenty years!"

And you know you've got to do something.

Mr. Sherman ("Mister" forever now, it seemed) was awake, but not quite alert: not alert like you have to be at work. He was up in the night again with his souvenirs and his demons. Outside, the components of a wonderful snowstorm were coming together, and there was a glowing bliss already gathering in his heart. He loved snow. At least, that's the way he remembered it.

In the black window, on the side with the forty-mile view in daytime, he could see a figure, backlit by the nightlight in the kitchen, its head a little crooked: tilted to one side, a gray fuzz spraying out from under a little flat hat. It was official: it was he.

Old English teachers talk that way, even after retirement. Everybody takes a little of his job with him when he goes, most likely. For him, it was predicate nominatives. It was *he.* (Has to be a nominative case pronoun. Old law.)

An old English teacher, then, retired now on his dreamed-of mountain, after the "wars" and the idiocy and the insanity, like one who fought in Korea or Viet Nam or the Gulf: noble, unbeaten, but a remnant of a thrown fight!

It was indeed he, out of bed and away from Wifey, out in the empty part of the house: quiet, and mucking about wondering whether to regret quitting early or to rejoice over being able to do it at all, and whether he was supposed to have died in the fight. Should he have kept on working? Could he have done more? Was the whole move a good idea? That sort of thing.

And then there was gas, too, and indigestion, and headache; for he had long since passed that nasty moment when the same food that once produced muscle and energy suddenly produced nothing but fat and gas. Unfair. Nobody had said anything, good or bad, about the fairness angle.

And there was the other doubt: the career doubt. Was he ever any good at what he did? He remembered mistakes. And he had a feeling there were lots of living rooms like this, with old guys from all professions and trades, pacing, flat-footed and a little lost. (Of course, few of them had the great view. Pity. Wifey had engineered a good buy.)

Running amok among night sweats in recent months, Mr. Sherman had discovered strange capabilities on the fringes of consciousness. He found that he could halt a nightmare short of disaster, if need be: stop a fall, save himself from embarrassment, dodge a bullet. He could stop a dream, get up and go pee, then return to finish the dream: repeat it, revise it, repair it, or toss it aside. He could choose a theme; he could hob-nob with celebrities; he could wake up and continue a dream as a fantasy. Nice. He just couldn't sleep. And the teaching dreams—frequent now, often messy or terrifying—were unmanageable. There was no real sleep.

But this night, he had decided, was going to be different. He had been handling it all wrong, trying to get back to sleep somehow. Tonight he would stay up and watch the snow—and fight his disturbing flashbacks toe to toe.

It was not supposed to be this way. On a night like this he should have been over there in the recliner with a good book. That was the original plan. He was going to go off into the hills and read every damn thing he could get his hands on: all the wonderful books he had missed while grading god-awful mounds of research papers and themes and letters and sketches all those years. But Mr. Sherman did not read anymore: he found that he did not enjoy it. Reading had become hard work. There had been 180 research papers toward the end there. That stack of papers haunted him now—chased him around the house! These days he shamelessly chipped away at GABB (*The Great American Bathroom Book*)—a good source of platitudes and plots, trivia and tripe. And alliteration. And when he was finished, he was finished, not with a flare but a flush. Pathetic.

Even Steinbeck. He could not even pick up a Steinbeck novel to beat back the insomnia or the insanity or whatever this was. He had always been able to make a lifelong reader of a kid by hooking him on Steinbeck. Worked every time. But now he himself could not sit down and read.

None of the irony of all this escaped Mr. Sherman, for irony was part of his baliwick. Knowing what it was called did not ease the pain.

So, this night, the weather, not reading, would be the

joyful distraction. And it all tied together, somehow. It was not because he was a "Homesick Eskimo" (as a southern colleague had once called him) that he loved snow. He had corrected his friend at the time, gently: "Homesick Eskimo" was not politically correct and still isn't; the term "Minnesota-American" would be accurate and acceptable. For the last twenty-seven years of his career he had taught English at Hugh Stone High School in a big southern city where there was only one season. These days, however, he stood in the middle of the continent where a full array of seasons paraded through "in all their glory," and tonight there would be snow. And snow was good, because when there's snow there's no school. Not if you do it right. Okay, it was too late to help him personally, but he reserved the right to rejoice for all those who still had to get up and go to work.

Hey, take your joy where you can find it, right?

Mr. Sherman poured up a Diet Coke and stared out the window. His experience with such nights had taught him that when he shut his eyes he would be bombarded with images like that stack of research papers, or like the sickening sound made when he snapped that little Iranian kid's back in the main hallway by the boys' restroom, or that flawless girl who made hugging raids during sexual harassment season! Or maybe Miss Whitby, his "mentee," would roll through with her stolen Safeway grocery cart, or kids might faint or have seizures, or some crazy parent might be after him—or the villagers! Or the hundreds of other "horrid images" (*Macbeth*, gang) that made sleep impossible. No, tonight he would do some caffeine, stay up, and sort it all out once and for all. Tomorrow he would be cured. Almost certainly.

Somewhere, deep in the bowels of the school district's absurd administrative building, there had to be a secret room, Mr. Sherman decided. To keep the madness away on these wild nights, and to keep from taking it all personally, he tried to imagine what it must have been like in that room when the

Think Tank met with its leader, Ol' Billy Joe Jim Bob Willie Wayne Kline.

Oh, the Think Tank was there, all right. It had to be. Like the thing in the garage that knots up electrical cords and tangles garden hoses. Like the force that blocks your path when you are in a hurry. Like the fiend that hides whatever you need right now! Everyone agreed that the crap that rained down on the schools—the catastrophic lunacy—had to be planned: systematic, plotted, intentional. You could feel them there, scheming, down in their secret room with the rats.

Mr. Sherman stared out the window, rather dramatically, he thought, and let his eyes relax—like when you're looking at one of those computer generated 3-D pictures. And then, gradually, he could see The Bastards. And the therapy began.

"Y'all set down now. We got us a new member—replacement for Ol' Ernie Carson here, who's been scarfed up by the guv'ment's Filthy Tricks division." He would set his huge Stetson down on the big table, probably, and adjust his string tie, and sit down—heavily. A guy like this would be big and sweaty, Mr. Sherman decided. "The Think Tank meeting is now in session."

Mr. Sherman imagined Ol' Billy Joe rapping for order with the butt of his Colt 45. He was an imposing man, the highly-paid superintendent of the biggest school district imaginable—a By-God empire! But this rotten Think Tank creation of his operated outside the actual district, without the knowledge of the school board, like so many things. No one could prove that it existed, but you just knew it was there.

"Ahmo innerduce Mister Harmon Bullington, rat cheer," he said. "Ol' Harm ain't got his doctorate yit, but we gonna fix him right up."

Now, Ol' Billy Joe et cetera was from L.A., but in the South, that wouldn't play. "Folks might not cotton to no Californy-types tellin' 'em what to do." Thus the phony accent. It would not be learned that he was from California until his retirement, or his alleged retirement. All of which made it particularly disgusting for Mr. Sherman to imagine in retrospect.

"We gonna come up with some kinda program that the district and mebbe the guv'ment can be conned into throwin' some money at—somethin' that'll snow the PTA, give the press a field day, hit a nerve with the NEA, and really piss off the teachers. An Ol' Harm Bullington's gonna be the Stud Buzzard!"

And then there would be the part where the new guy would play dumb, like the character in the old sci-fi movies who kept saying, "Gee, Professor, how does that work?" (Do not mock sci-fi movies. Some great teaching there!) Anyway, this Harmon Bullington fellow would say, "I do need a Ph.D., but for the life of me, I cannot imagine how you can help me."

"Stay tuned, Son. See, yer here to think up dirty stuff—absolutely vile trash! Think set-up/disappointment; think broken promise, injustice, ingratitude, programmed stupidity. Y'all cain't be thinkin' somethin' as screwed-up as this school system just happens! Somebody gets drunk, thinks it up, writes it down, and gets a Ph.D. It's the law."

And then he would introduce the others at the table. His favorite word would be 'Sears. "'Sears ma wahf, Ol' Minnie Mae Lizbutt Marie Kline, Ph.D." She would be a severe little lady with blue hair and silver chains on her glasses, and she would wear suits—business suits. On the side she would have a business selling babies or stealing Social Security benefits or something like that.

"Now Minnie Mae here is the person who thought up the whole 'Dumb Down' program. We call her *Doctor* Minnie Mae these days."

And then Minnie Mae—Ol' Minnie Mae—doctor—would explain how, when The Press started complaining about illiteracy and poor math skills—the results of earlier deliberate programs and Ph.D.'s—she came up with Dumbing Down the whole curriculum.

"But how," Harmon Bullington would ask, right on cue, "did you ever get the educators to go along with that?"

And then Ol' Minnie Mae would get a look like the wife of The Grinch would probably have, and she would deliver! "We blamed the tests. We blamed Iowa and Princeton for coming up with tests that a poor city kid just could not possibly pass—tests that required both skill and knowledge. We said city kids had special needs, had to have special teaching, special tests. And this would take special teachers who (now get this) who really cared!"

"And, Son, if you wanna piss a teacher off, just imply that she doesn't care! Doctor Minnie Mae here had'em thinkin' it was real special to slow it all down, make it all fun, lower the requirements and expectations, take away all the effort and competition . . ."

"So the teachers got the message that they should dumb it down, but you never really said to do that?"

"They's no written order anywhere! By God, this boy's smarter'n ah thought. Ol' Minnie Mae Ph.D. had them teachers comin' up with this crap themselves! They gave each other awards fer it; some of 'em dressed up like Mother Goose and spoon fed them ghetto hoods like they was total idjuts. It didn't take long to make school so damn easy a pumpkin could get a diploma in two years."

"Of course," Doctor Minnie Mae intoned, "they wouldn't be able to make change for a dollar—or read their diploma. Ah, sweetness!"

"And all that was your idea, Minnie Mae?" asked Harm.

"That's Doctor Minnie Mae. I got my Ph.D. using the district's statistics—a half-million kids and all those teachers throbbing away. My thesis was called, *Expecting Less*: an analysis of the dumb-ass dipstick kids . . ."

But the fantasy was interrupted by a horrible cracking sound, and Mr. Sherman was yanked away from the Think Tank meeting, back through the kitchen, and into the main hallway outside the boys' bathroom and one of the defining moments of his career. He was suddenly breaking the little Iranian boy's neck again.

A fist fight had been rolling through the main hall—several years ago—around noon, as Mr. Sherman recalled, amid two thousand kids on the move between classes. It was your standard, off-the-rack fist fight: feet & fists, mainly. As usual, the rules for intervention were clear: 1) Stop the fight; 2) Stop the fight before it breaks out; 3) Do not touch anyone; 4) Do not raise your voice; 5) Do not get hit; 6) Place yourself between the combatants; 7) Call for help; 8) Talk to the temporarily confused angelic children in a polite manner, convincing them not to kill one another . . . Well, you get the idea.

And so Mr. Sherman had walked up behind the Iranian kid, the smaller of the two temporarily confused angelic children, and wrapped his arms around the kid and pulled him away from the other kid, who was really kicking ass. A coach put the other boy up against the wall with force. And then Mr. Sherman's kid struggled. And Mr. Sherman squeezed.

There was a sickening, bony "Karraack!" that vibrated all through the kid's body and Mr. Sherman's—that sounded like the moment in martial arts movies when someone in black pajamas twists an inconsequential drone's neck and snaps it. And that is a sound that can still pull Mr. Sherman away from a nightmare, a daydream, making love, even eating pizza: a sound that is in his soul forever.

Disturbing. All this time had passed, and he was out of there and safely retired on his mountain with a nice snowstorm on the way, fantasizing about The Bastards in the Think Tank, and he could still be yanked silly by that hideous sound. All it was this time was the house contracting in the cold. But once you've broken a kid, you come down with some sort of syndrome.

Oh, nothing was actually broken: no back, no neck, no spinal column. Mr. Sherman had just given the kid's back a nice cracking, like a chiropractor would. He immediately set the kid down, and the kid ran off into the thousands of reeking, grinning numbskulls, and it was over. Over. Except for the sound. It could have been the sound of the end of Mr. Sherman as a teacher, unless he cared to tutor fellow convicts in the slammer.

Mr. Sherman noticed that, cold and shivering as he was, as he always was when he heard that sound, he was sweating. He focused on his reflection in the black window. "That which we are, we are," he said out loud. A little Tennyson, he remembered. And then he willfully turned his mind toward happier thoughts.

Mr. Sherman had always been called Mister—well, ever since his first day as a teacher when he was twenty-one. He had even gone with girls who called him Mister. Mister. But the pronoun used by The Press when mentioning teachers had always been "she"—or "her." Teachers were women to the public. You could pay them less because of that. It was women's work, after all. But Mr. Sherman had lived and taught during the liberation fad, and the money had trickled down—not like in private industry, but better than before. So he rode in on the ladies' horse, hooked up with the big city district, made good enough money to retire before 60 and head for the hills. Bless that retirement system and tax-sheltered annuities! Those were the good thoughts. They were also the sad ones.

And then his focus changed, and Ol' Billy Joe et cetera was introducing another member of the Think Tank.

"'Sears mah ol' buddy, Ernie Carson, Ph.D., outgoing culprit in charge of TSF's."

"Glad to meet you, Doctor. But what does TSF mean, if I might ask?"

Mr. Sherman loved how stupid that sounded, but he just knew it had to be that way. Dr. Ernie Carson would look like the problem: fat, squinty-eyed, drooling, "Vacancy" sign on his forehead.

"Put 'er there, Harm! You gonna have my job, an' Ah gonna go over to Washington. You gonna be the new TSF man in this here school district, so pay attention. TSF means 'Teacher Stress Factor,' Son."

Ernie would talk exactly like Ol' Billy Joe et cetera, Mr. Sherman decided. Why complicate it? It was only a fantasy anyway. Up in the night with these miseries, he sought to simplify.

"Now, Son, Ernie was the best TSF man we ever had. As his replacement, it will be your job to guage the TSF potency of each outrage we suggest or set up. It's how much you piss 'em off that is important here! Now, something like Mainstreaming, where we had little sick kids put into school with the normies: that was a 9.7 on the one-to-ten scale. Then we came up with labeling ever kid that stepped out of line A.D.D.—Attention Deficit Disorder. That was a Ten!"

Ol' Billy Joe et cetera would naturally offend just about everybody. "Someday ah'll tell y'all how we set up that scale," he told Bullington.

"You got to learn to compound the insults, too, Son. Best thing to do is tell 'em what's wrong, and then tell 'em what's right—only they the same thing!! That'll drive 'em nuts."

"For instance?" said Harmon Bullington.

Ol' Billy Joe et cetera leaned back, lifted up a dirty Diet Coke can, and spit a sloppy black cud into it and then swabbed his tongue around his mouth very visibly. "Hell, ah cain't even remember the name o' the boy that got his Ph.D. fer this, but Sexual Harassment was the theme o' the thing. By God, we had 'em jumpin' on that one. Whole idea was there was no way to win. Sexual Harassment was bad and you could get fahrd. Only thing was, just about anything anybody, male or female or undecided, did, was sexual harassment by definition."

"Anything y'all said or did wuz bad," Ernie added. "And we duped the teachers into naming their own poison. You shoulda seen it. We'd git the whole faculty of a school together and have a meeting. Penalize the coaches fer missin' it. Then we'd tell 'em we had this problem and we needed their hep to solve it, and we split 'em up into color-coded groups."

"Racial groups?"

"Hell no. But that woulda pissed 'em off, too. No, we jist handed out pieces of paper of various colors. The ones who got kiwi would go to a corner, the cranberry bunch would go to another corner, the mango to another . . ."

"The blacks to another corner?"

"God no! Didn't go there. You couldn't have a black group 'cuz people would have thought it symbolic. No, jist everthin' but black and white. So, anyway, they would run off in all directions, sayin' 'I'm a kiwi, I'm a kiwi!'"

"It was freakin' circus! We used to video tape 'em. It was a By-God scream! God, ahmo miss this job," said Ernie.

"Y'all sure y'all wanna go now? Y'all never have that kind o' fun in Washinton, Son."

"Oh, I'm committed now. Anyway, back to the story. The teachers would run off in all directions and set down in tight circles and make up lists of things they thought someone might think was Sexual Harassment. Ten or twelve groups would come in later with eight or nine things on their lists, and we'd have 'em put it all down on a piece of butcher paper with a big slobbery marker and hang it on the wall!"

"'Member: they like crap like that! It's what they call 'Inneractive'—and that, we convinced 'em, was real good! So, we'd end up with one giant list of things they thought wuz Sexual Harassment."

"Then what?"

"Then we threw all that trash away and they'd forget the whole damn thing. But then we'd send 'em a bulletin that summarized it all: any touchy-feely stuff was automatically suspect. At the same time we'd get 'em to write down what they thought a good teacher wuz, and that's where you'd get 'em!"

"Be sensitive! Be warm! Be friendly! Be curious! Be sympathetic! Be available! Be empathetic! Hand out condoms! Make contact! Give them love."

"Jist don't touch nobody, look directly at nobody, get into nobody's business, show *any* favoritism . . . ! Had 'em comin' and goin', Son! It was *my* idea, ah'm proud to say." Carson straightened and looked wistfully at something far away and said, "Ah luv the smell of frustration at a faculty meeting."

"Son," said Ol' Billy Joe et cetera, "them's the shoes you got to fill."

Another terrifying image shut off that meeting, and Mr. Sherman was sweating again. This time it was Velma, a beautiful black girl who needed hugs and decided that Mr. Sherman, standing at his door, was a good target. She had transferred in from a nearby school district where hugs were being distributed. Hugs were simply the big thing at that school at that time. It was deemed in one of *their* meetings that students might hit each other less, shoot each other less, cut or stab each other less, if they all got hugged more. So they were hugging at Velma's school when she transferred to Hugh Stone High. The problem was that Sexual Harassment was the current mania at Hugh Stone High, and hugging was definitely on the taboo list. Both lists, actually. And there was dumpy old Mr. Sherman, standing by his door.

"Velma, please do not hug me," his arms straight out to the sides, like Christ on the cross.

"Why? Can't you take it, Mr. Sherman?"

"I assure you it is a most effective hug, Velma, but it is inappropriate."

"But I like you! What's wrong with a hug? I hug my dad, my grandpa . . ."

"But if you hug me, it could be the end of my career, my marriage, my reputation, my life, and the world as we know it."

Mr. Sherman knew that the Think Tank did not want him hugged by any pretty girl. An ugly girl perhaps, or, just for kicks, a boy student. That would make them howl. But not Velma. Not at Hugh Stone High.

"Is it because I'm black?"

"No, it's because you are beautiful."

"Now *you're* hitting on *me*!"

"I am not. Disengage, Velma, and go into the room. Sit. Relax."

"But I don't have you this period!"

"Then go to class, please!"

Fortunately, the lady teacher across the hall helped out by explaining to the girl that, although Velma might find Mr. Sherman sexless as an anemic nun (Sinclair Lewis—Minnesota boy), the world would not see it that way, and the hug would be trouble. And the girl backed off. But Mr. Sherman still had night sweats about it.

He looked again at his reflection in the black window. "I stayed hugged, though," he admitted. "The kid could hug."

"So," he thought, "nothing really bad has actually happened to me." He had developed this worry-wart routine all on his own. After all, he had done what everybody really wants to do: he had gone into the rat race, eked out a living, put aside some money, and retired to a peaceful mountain top while young enough to appreciate it. "Lighten up, Mister Sherman!"

The name Sherman had gone over well at Confederate States of America's Hugh Stone High, as can be imagined. Hugh Stone High was named after an obscure general who had served under Robert E. Lee during the Civil War, no one was sure how far down under. But in front of the school, the Confederate flag flew right under the American flag; the teams were called The Rebels; the school song was *Dixie*; the newspaper was named *Yee-Hah*!—well, you get the picture. Of course, there was a huge stone out front, too. For the North, General Sherman had trampled the South to mush and walked the puddle dry, and the name Sherman was not amusing to these people. Not until there was a big population shift in that part of town, and suddenly 45% of the kids were African Americans. Not only that, but Hispanic and Asian kids showed up, too—lots of them. Kids from all over the globe came aboard. Something had to be done.

"Ahmo tull y'all what's got to be done," the Think Tank was told. Probably. "We gonna hatch ideas here, and we gonna do it now! Minnie Mae?"

"That's Doctor Minnie Mae. I say we poll the students. That should take a full day—just figuring out the form. Then we could test 'em on the Civil War, geography, and personality. We could have a psychological test to ferret out the rednecks, do a foreign word recognition test . . ."

"Okay, that'll git us through to June. But whut we gonna do next fall?"

"I have it," said Harmon Bullington. "We start the year with a whole mess of screwball exercises in what we'll call 'tolerance.' Now, 'tolerance' is a word that implies that something is a little hard to swallow, so it'll have maximum TSF pointage right away—insult the hell out of a lot of people. We'll take class time—out of English and math—to bounce these kids off each other as whatever they are: Black, Chinese, Mexican, Eskimo . . ."

"Hot damn! y'all onto somethin' there! We could have 'em fill out a lot o' forms admittin' what they are—with initials like W and B and O and NA . . ."

"NA? Not applicable?'

"No. Native Amercian, Boy. Gotta git the Redskins in there! And, like y'all say, in English and Math classes. Then we'll jump all over them English and Math teachers fer not teachin'."

"And, in the end, everyone would be offended by just about everyone else. Then we could make the kids come up with a better idea: divide 'em up into groups . . ."

"Color-coded groups. Butcher paper!"

"And 'share.' Don't forget sharing," Minnie Mae would put in there. "The teachers like to share things. It's one of their words: they get a peculiar light in their eyes when someone says 'share.' Did we do that?"

"Don't remember."

"But then we could pass out a whole mess of crystal apples and crap to reward 'em. We got a deal on a big bunch of crystal apples, and they'll fight over 'em. Beats the hell out of money. Damn! I like it!" And Bill Joe et cetera would let fly a nasty brown cud.

Well, in the end, a wonderful transition was made at the school. They renamed their mascot (Johnny Reb) and called him 'Rocky'; the school song became "Like a Rock"; the newspaper's name was changed to *The Pebble* . . . Well, you get the idea. Seven teachers got crystal apples and four got honorable mentions. For a while, life was good.

As one of the new kids put it, "Is was to be like as to when neighborhood."

Mr. Sherman could not help but take a few moments out of the night to consider all the good things about teaching. June was good, and July, and August. Christmas vacation was good, Spring Break, Thanksgiving Vacation. President's Day and Martin Luther King Day. Bless 'em. Bless 'em all. And snow vacations. But snow vacations were not for the South. Hurricane days, though! Those were good! And closure. That, he concluded, was the best thing about teaching: you have closure. There comes a time each semester when you total up the scores, feed it all to the computer, and close your books. You go away free, and nothing can be done about it at all. You let go, and it's over for a while. It's closure that keeps teachers alive.

And then there's Friday afternoon.

Always, in his darkest moments, in the longest of ordeals, there had been the Friday Afternoon Margarita Meeting. Maybe not always, but time before the Margarita meetings was no longer important. It was an answer to the Think Tank. If they could have one at the administration building, there could be one off campus in a seedy little dark bar after hostilities on Friday. Whether or not the Think Tank was real, this was real. For the last few years of his career, Mr. Sherman had gone to that meeting. Every Friday, come Hell, high water, or the PTA, and at the slightest provocation, anytime!

Mr. Sherman was not, however, the founder. No, the guru, the Wizard, the sage, the leader—the Grand Kleegle—The Royal Omnipotent High Potentate Supreme—well, that was Jerry. And there was something about settling into that murky haven with Jerry and a giant Margarita that was a religious experience for Mr. Sherman. (Even Jerry called him Mister Sherman—a little private joke about dignity.) It was a session of therapy; it was confession; it was sanctuary. It was a place where it didn't seem as if The Bastards could get you. It was a place to interpret mixed messages, make sense of the madness, adjust to the indignities, absorb the outrage. Of all aspects of his career, including the kids, Mr. Sherman missed this the most.

Jerry liked the idea that history was just one damned thing after another—and *he* taught history. In his youth he had marched up and down with signs, protesting things. Now he looked like Santa Claus, sounded like Wilson (the guy over the back fence on *Home Improvement*), and wore like iron. There was nobody who remembered more cycles of the district's insanities—and no one better to hoist Margaritas with on a Friday afternoon after the last busload of "perps" had been hauled away from school.

And then there were the girls. Darby McTrain was a lady of Mr. Sherman's vintage who went by the book, no matter what. Period. Her favorite passtime was exposing the insanity of The Book. The gang called her Train Person. When the Think Tank put out the order that to solve problems of control and discipline at school every teacher must, without fail, stand by "her" door in the hallway between classes, Darby did it to the nth degree. If there was a fist fight, a fire, a coup d'etat, a rape, a revolution, a bombing—whatever at all—in her room, that was too bad: Darby McTrain was standing by her door in the hall. If students needed help, if the principal wanted to talk to her, if the Second Coming occured anywhere but by Darby's door, she did not attend. The gang frequently sang "Stand By Your Door" during the second Margarita. Darby drank soda, however—but then, she was quirky.

Another regular at the meeting was Colleen O'Hara, always just back from a trip to Ireland, as Mr. Sherman conjured her. All things Irish were part of that image, and beyond that, a teacher who worked one-on-one with anyone who really wanted to learn—endlessly, tirelessly. Sometimes, she would even be late for the Friday meeting, but she had the ability to catch up, no matter how far she was behind. And she always made Mr. Sherman wonder who Mr. Sherman was, as he wondered now.

Those were the core people. But there was something

else about the Margarita meeting. Any one of the core characters could arrive alone, early perhaps, and find the pathetic table there in the gloom, and hunker down and feel the weight of the world lift away. The drink would show up automatically, and, with both hands, with a sort of ceremonial, nurturing care, it would be lifted to the lips of the battered and beaten pilgrim, and Friday would come over the shattered soul. (Or something equally dramatic for sure.) Many times Mr. Sherman had been first, and alone.

Not alone like this night. And Diet Coke is no Margarita. Mr. Sherman looked at his reflection again, but this time he thought about Mother Teresa. Not that he looked like her or anything like her—or made anything like her contribution. Mother Teresa had worked well into her nineties and died in harness. Any number of others—John Glenn, Ronald Reagan, Helen Hayes, Andy Rooney, Benjamin Franklin—legions of them had kept on keeping on, and Mr. Sherman had hung up his red pencil before 60—handed the chalk over to a youngster—dropped out of school, quit, thrown in the towel, taken the pension and headed for open country. The former. The late great. The retired. The quitter. No longer. He half-way expected to hear a knock at the door, and open the door to find, standing there in the upcoming snow, a small committee of school administrators offering money, perks, boxes and boxes of crystal apples, if only he would return from his exile and, please, save another generation of American youth.

But it was not a knock that aroused Mr. Sherman from his revery: it was the "Karrack" again, and he was holding the body of an Iranian kid, limp and lifeless. But he looked down and it was not the Iranian kid at all: it was Velma, and it was a hug! The scream in his soul was the same, and the madness was complete.

"My God," he muttered, "I have got to fix this!"

Chapter Two

Mr. Sherman could fix almost anything. He had been in the South for Integration, after all—at work in the school. The country had no qualms about asking his generation of teachers to handle that one. He had officially felt the heat of the melting pot, and he assumed that someday, if the whole experiment came to be considered a failure, he would take part of the blame—even if The Bastards had to dig him up. When AIDS came along, his classroom was where kids were officially told that although this was an epidemic—a pandemic really—there was no danger in mere proximity at school—unless they happened to have sex and swap bodily fluids with someone. Yeah. Right. He had also tried to fix senior high school students who had not been taught to read or write in grade school or middle school. He intervened in suicides, seizures, runaways, fights—all the normal fare, like any teacher. So a little personal insanity seemed well within his scope.

He turned off the light in the kitchen. Now he could see out the black window without confronting his reflection, and that was less complicated. It narrowed his world. The past was complete, as some psychiatrist might say, and the future would take care of itself. He became aware of a gust of wind and movement among the bare limbs of the walnut tree close to the house. Cold sounds. Snow was coming. Mr. Sherman had an instinct about snow. Besides, the weathermen on three channels had been calling for snow all day long. A little data can sharpen instinct.

He decided that he would be pulling an all-nighter anyway, even if he had not quit. He would be plowing his way through a mound of illiteracy, trying to fix things: sentences that didn't work, spelling and grammar errors, continuity and parallelism problems. It would be like that time on the mountain, uphill out of Durango, that lonely Christmas between marriages. An all-nighter. Startling images: ice sliding down the A-Frame's roof; a snow-woman proportioned meticulously from memory; a stack of probably 170+ research papers; and a mound where he had parked his pathetic car. Oh, yes—a snow woman! Of course! You simply build a snowman and keep adding snow in key places. They are pleasing to the eye. They cannot grade papers, but they have a place. A teacher has all kinds of needs. She was a stone fox, too, this snow woman: By-God alabaster! And, later in the evening, she was the only human form he could see when he had great need of humanity. And the snow on that roof, zooming down the A-frame and hitting the bottom with a crack.

Yes, that crack. The kid's spine again, cracking in his merciless grip. The Iranian kid falling limp, his dead paralyzed legs dragging the floor in the main hall outside the boys' restroom. Variations on a death dance.

He hated it when that happened. Safe now and out of the loop, he was still assailed by potential souvenirs—of things that really hadn't quite happened. Fact was, he had always expected to go out in a blaze of infamy. They would get him on something. They had promised.

"We gonna make it damn near impossible, folks." It was Ol' Billy Joe et cetera's voice, so he tried the focus trick again. Dr. Billy Joe et cetera must have had a hand in planning this one, but he gave the credit, rather graciously, to Ol' Ernie Carson, Ph.D. "Son, y'all jist gotta tell the girls about this thing yer doin'"

And then Ol' Ernie got up—reared up like a cobra. "The area of Assessment has been neglected to the point where it's practically fair, and we cain't have that! Ah have determined that, as part o' what we will call Pre-Assessment, we will require that each teacher meet with an administrator and name her own worst weakness. She will then address that weakness with a 'Growth Program' in which she jumps through some hoops and supposedly repairs her weakness. Teachers luv to fix things. So we'll do all kinds o' crazy stuff with 'em—and write it all down in their records."

"We could probably design a test for that," offered Ol' Doctor Minnie Mae.

"Just wait! Lissen to the Boy here! Give 'em the grabber, Son."

"On the next evaluation or assessment or whatever we call it at the time, we'll have the administrator say, 'Hmmmm. Miss Brown, I cain't hep noticin' that y'all had a big problem with yer Self-Control a while back! Anything I should know?"

"Now ain't that By-God brilliant? Self-Control could mean all kinds of twisted, sexual crap—or violent temper tantrums, or language problems—swearin' & cussin' & usin' the Lord's name in vain . . ."

"Oh, yeah! And 'Classroom Management' (one of our other categories) could mean they couldn't teach, and 'Subject Matter' could mean they didn't know their field. Trick is, you get THEM to come up with their own Achilles' heel, and then you use it to stress them to death!"

General applause among the members of the Think Tank.

"Son, this arrives just in time fer the Merit Pay wars. The damn 'Board is insistin' that we give out some merit pay. It won't happen fer a couple of years, but we gonna have this in place by then. Ever one of 'em will have been on a growth program, and we can say, 'Darn darn darn, Miss Sweet Thing, Ah see y'all been strugglin' with homosexuality—and chalk dust stains.'"

Mr. Sherman had gone for that one, and he knew about it. He had signed up for a Growth Program in "Self-Control"—because it was required and seemed the easiest. He invented paragraphs of utter bullroar that sounded like a growth program, and then he handed it in and forgot it. Two years later, a new Assessor was in the house, the original having retired to her mountain. And the new one looked across the table and said, "Hmmmm, I can't help noticing that you had trouble with your self-control a while back. Merit Pay does not go to people who have been on a growth program in the last three years. You will have to wait a year. Pity, really." That was the day Mr. Sherman became certain that a Think Tank was there somewhere, composting, rotting, seething, festering, fermenting . . .

But this was a new day, and Mr. Sherman felt a sudden wave of inspiration hit him broadside. He resented being so vulnerable to these terrors so long after the fact. The past is dead. The Past is over: release it. The Past is Prologue. But if teachers can fix anything, why not the past? It was so simple, really: he could use this time, this wakeful nightmare of insomnia, this all-night fit of horrible imaginings—to repair the past, to put it right. He could become the hero of his life, snatch victory from the jaws of pedagogy, and solidify his sanity—perhaps before morning!

He would now seek out his demons: invite them, summon them, drag them out and make the necessary improvements.

"Miss Whitby," he bellowed, "Front and center!"

When every classroom in Hugh Stone High, including "shacks" on campus, had been occupied by a teacher and a class or by one of the scores of offices that seemed to be spreading through the building like some kind of infestation, it was time for a diabolical stunt. Mr. Sherman was not sure who was the primary source of this, but the Think Tank was behind it without a doubt.

Miss Whitby, a black girl just out of college and conspicuously the most energetic, dedicated, enthusiastic and talented young teacher possible, was brought in one October morning to "help out around the school." Since there was no classroom for her, she "floated"—which meant that she occupied a room vacated by a teacher on her free period. Miss Whitby had six rooms, then, spread out all over the building—two wings, three floors, full city block, enough room for 2400 kids. And she was given "overflow" students: the dregs, the outcasts, the scum-bags—just like in the movies. She stood four foot eleven, and her textbooks were two and a half inches thick. She got around with a stolen Safeway grocery cart and an elevator key given up by a wheelchair student who had transferred out. And she was Mr. Sherman's mentee.

"You will be her mentor, Mr. Sherman," said the principal.

"Okay. What does that mean? Am I her boss?"

"No. Her mentor. You help her."

"Good. Am I in charge of her? Do I train her?"

"No. You are her mentor. You will help smooth things over for her . . ."

"Get her a room? Make sure she has fair class sizes? Get the criminals out of her classes?"

"Not really . . ."

"Show her the ropes? Give her advice? Tell her where the bodies are buried?"

"Something like that . . ."

"Am I a role model here? I could show her what it's like

to be a white guy with 35 years of experience, nearing retirement. Just tell me what mentoring is, and I'll mentor the hell out of her."

In a truly huge district, they handle things like this efficiently. Mr. Sherman found himself in the ballroom of a large hotel with all of the mentors from all of the schools in the district. They were split up into smaller, color-coded groups and scattered over the hotel. Mr. Sherman was with the cranberry group that time.

"I demand that Miss Whitby be given a stolen WalMart grocery cart ASAP!" Mr. Sherman should have said firmly. "Two of the wheels on her stolen Safeway cart are flat—nearly square—and it's a scandal! A teacher at Hugh Stone High may not be able to have a decent room or decent students, but, by thunder, she is entitled to a quality stolen grocery cart!"

Now that was a repair worth making. Mr. Sherman had felt very guilty about being of no use to Miss Whitby at all. He had never marched into the main office, locked eyeballs with the principal, and demanded a better life for Miss Whitby! But he could fix that now. If the ghosts could walk through his midnights, he had a license to tamper!

"I further demand that she be given a crystal apple in advance. The girl wants to teach more than anybody I have seen in years. It is her passion: she wants to touch humanity, shape young minds, make a difference. And you've got her running around the halls like a bag lady in Brooklyn. She spent yesterday afternoon locked in an elevator!"

"Mr. Sherman, this is not what a mentor does."

"Piffle!" he should have told them, mashing his fist down into a pile of discipline cards on the principal's desk. "Piffle. Piffle."

Yeah, right. Maybe he could have told her about his own experiences as a young black female teacher just out of college and five feet tall flung into boiling caldron of drugs and hormones. Possibly not.

Oh, well. Miss Whitby is an E-worker these days, somewhere in that city of one season. The kids drove her out. If she was not respected enough to have a classroom, who was she anyway? That's the way the kids put it, and said it to her face—seasoned with the customary profanities. She left Hugh Stone High and all schools forever. And grocery carts still bother Mr. Sherman, mentor.

He knew now, however, that fixing the Miss Whitby thing would be a simple matter of re-remembering the details. It is done all the time, so why not for the sake of sanity?

But it also occured to him that before this night was over, he would have to go one-on-one with Ol' Billy Joe Jim Bob Willie Wayne Kline himself. Possibly the whole Think Tank.

He could hear them crowing. "Lissen up, Boy! Ahmo tell y'all how we shucked this li'l lady fresh outa college. Nailed her in a semester and a half! Hell, she was a By-God masterpiece." He would tell the whole story about driving Miss Whitby out of the system, and about her valiant struggle. "We had her buyin' her own books! She wanted them black kids to read some books they could identify with, so she went out and bought 'em and hauled 'em all over that school in a stolen grocery cart—late everywhere she went! When she went to the bathroom, they stole the books and the wheels to the cart, eventually the whole cart. Said she had been "dissed" by the system and why should they care! Damn, Boy, it was beautiful. Kicker is, we fixed her up with a powerless mentor—gutless wonder, probably worried about his retirement! Then we gave HIM a crystal apple for being a mentor!"

Someday, Mr. Sherman would get that crystal apple out of the box under the bed in the spare room and use it for target practice. If he could figure out which crystal apple that was.

The more he looked at the situation, however, the more he liked Miss Whitby just the way she was: idealistic, noble, smart, dedicated—just what she should be!—and gone, too. Just as she naturally would be. Bless her.

"Y'all got to git the big picture here, Son. If they git the idea they're valuable—like they doin' some good—hell, they jist want money. Y'all gotta keep 'em off balance with conflictin' signals and impossible sitchiations!"

"Gee, Professor, what ever do you mean?" (This would be earlier in Harmon Bullington's orientation process at the Think Tank.)

"Yuh come up with a doozy—like the New Math! Remember that, Minnie Mae? Y'all git a Ph.D. fer somebody fer comin' up with it, but you make sure the teachers 'implement' it. Teachers love to 'implement'—love the word! They like 'ownership' and 'empowerment' too. 'I own that! I am so empowered by that!' Damn simpletons. Anyway, New Math fell on its face cuz they couldn't do the old math, we told The Press, and they run off hollerin' 'What's wrong with these teachers anyway?' God, I loved it so!"

"Hardly seems fair. I like it. I'm going to love this job, Dr. Billy Joe et cetera."

Ol' Billy Joe et cetera would mentor that Bullington person. "Ah wuz a figger juggler when I started up, Son. Learned to press-whip them figgers. We put out the myth that there was one teacher fer ever 22 kids. The Press bought it hook, line, and sinker, and printed it fer the truth. What we did was, we took all the janitors, librarians, cooks, secretaries, and Special ED officers, added 'em up, and combined that with the number of teachers. Then we divided that into the number of kids. The answer was 22. Hell, boy, we had 35 kids in damn near ever required class out there! Yuh gotta *think* with us, Boy!"

"Well, how about hall monitors?"

"That's the spirit, Son. Damn, you gonna be good at this crap."

The image of 180 research papers, ungraded and

probably undocumented, stacked high and reeking, slammed into Mr. Sherman's mind once again. But the Regulator clock with the screwed-up hour hand struck 12:17 and saved him.

"Good Grief," he muttered. "The night is young."

Mr. Sherman had been in on the whole decline and fall of public schools in America, now that he thought about it. Hugh Stone High had been one of the best in the district back when he signed up. He had moved into the city from a small town out in the corn belt, where he had taught English and drama and speech, and he had worked in the private sector for six whole months; but then he had crawled back into Education, into the classroom, thinking there was honor in it. He reasoned that one day, from his death bed, he could look back on a teaching career and ahead to the gates of Heaven and expect to be welcomed into the next life, a hero of this one. These days, after a 27-year hitch in the city system, he no longer believed in public education, in himself, or in God—much.

"It's just a phase I'm going through," he said out loud. "It's going to snow, and I'll feel better in the morning."

As he looked out into the night, he thought of the first time he had seen a school bus crawling along the mountain road two or three miles over across the canyon—a yellow light flashing in the pre-dawn darkness. "Poor devils," he had thought, "heading for school already and the sun isn't even up yet." That was a good moment. This was a good moment. This was a morning when he was not going to roll out and head over to the local font of teenage enlightenment and flail away. True appreciation of retirement swept over him. And then the doubt.

Doubt and guilt. This doubt, and this guilt, here and now, this night on this promised mountain. "By morning, when I look out there and we've got snow, I will beat this thing. I have earned this life, and I am going to enjoy it: day and night," Mr. Sherman said infirmly with both doubt and guilt.

Something in the realm of a ten on the toxicity scales was happening in Mr. Sherman's gut. He thought about a nice warm bowl of Rolaids with a Maalox topping, and Tums for after-dinner mints. But that would put low-grade cement in the lower tract, and then he would be into laxatives. Ulcers were caused by a virus now, according to CNN, and no virus could stay alive in these mountains. So it was probably just angina or a hiatal hernia or acid reflux. Or maybe just dinner. He took another sip of Diet Coke.

"It's the guilt," he admitted. "I let 'em get away with it, and they let me get away with it, too."

A sudden chill struck Mr. Sherman, and he grabbed a garish serape from the couch and put his head through the slit and made the adjustments. He picked up his reflection, and the effect was comic: his little flat hat with the multicolored blanket seemed ludicrous. "Hmmm. a variegated graduate? Or, not."

Whenever he had been forced to wear the cap and gown, the seriousness of the moment had made him nervous. Something akin to stage fright had gripped him. Would he fall down? Would he goof up, go for the laugh, and ruin the somber occasion? The ceremonies were part of getting out of school, receiving the diploma or the degree, and they were probably necessary. Parents and grand parents, teachers or professors or dignitaries: all were watching. It was true that he had formally requested that he be excused from the Masters Ceremonies, but his request had been denied and he had been forced to go to the proper place at the proper time and wear the cap and gown and get the diploma, just like the others. And he had gotten through it with some semblance of dignity.

Then he had attended the beautiful, emotional commencement ceremonies in small-town Nebraska and Iowa: solemn, powerful, not-a-dry-eye-in-the-house sort of thing, full of meaning: proud observers who were used to watching things slowly grow, mature, ripen.

At Hugh Stone High, things were different.

At sporting arenas and rinks all over the city, the legions of graduates from the district's many high schools thundered through "the Walk" and received their diplomas in ceremonies that had their own special character. When the principal was a male, he was handed a marble in exchange for each and every diploma—six hundred marbles in the earlier days! More like four hundred later, after The System took hold and fewer kids actually stayed for the end. If the principal was a woman, she might receive condoms—or eggs! Tradition is good, probably.

Commencement included a massive squirt-gun fight in those earlier days—which escalated to fights with those large "soaker" weapons later. You just prayed for water, because there was wine to be had, and grape juice, and lighter fluid. And acid. And bleach. The caps and gowns were not the drab weeds of the midwest schools, black or blue. No, *mango* was in, and *kiwi*, and *cranberry*, and *puce*. And there were decals and signs, yards of "honor cords" and other trinkets. Face painting was popular. Glue and glitter. And under the gowns, bikinis or boxers, or just kids. You hated to look, and, if you pulled graduation detail, you had to look. Shower shoes at the bottom of the ensemble, of course.

In the stands, the parents screamed and stamped their feet, rent the air with compressed-air horns, bounced beach balls around the stands and into the graduate formations, performed "the wave"—and generally re-enacted Mardi Gras or some political convention demonstration. Sometimes they booed the principal or the guest speaker.

Mr. Sherman's outfit would have fit right in, except the serape was more dignified.

The graduates would "walk," all right, and then go forth into the world—or fifth, or sixth . .

"Hot Damn, Boy! Ah luv it when a plan comes together!" Brimstone. Red smoke.

"Am I leaving too early, Jerry?"

"Hmmm. That's your call, my friend. Still, history is full of folks who stayed too long. Custer comes to mind. Stayed too long at Little Big Horn. Mussolini hung around Italy too long; Captain Smith probably wished he could break tradition and get off the Titanic a little earlier . . ."

"Right. And there was Lincoln at the theater, Caesar at the forum, old Harry Truman at St. Helens . . ."

"Hishimata at Hiroshima . . ."

"I've never heard of him."

"See there? Stayed too long!"

"Sick."

"Should have left earlier—no question about it."

"Here's to Hishimata—and all who stayed too long!"

And there would be the customary toast with the Friday Margarita. Fun and games, making fun of tragedy . .

"Hold it. Seriously, now, Mr. Sherman: There is a National disaster going on here, and you and I are right in the middle of it. When it's complete, this country is not going to blame Progressive Education or New Math or Dr. Spock or John Dewey."

"They're going to blame the teachers: you and me."

"And Miss Whitby. They blamed soldiers for Viet Nam—called 'em names. No, you're not leaving too early. Only God and other teachers will know the truth. So go to that mountain."

Chapter Three

Scuz-bag lawyers on TV keep saying that a defendant who is his own attorney has a fool for a client. It must be true, thought Mr. Sherman, that a disturbo who was his own psychiatrist was probably crazy. Same thing. But, as a teacher he could never have considered being seen with a psychiatrist, even if the HMO picked up the tab—well, especially if the HMO picked up the tab.

"We gonna offer 'em counseling fer free," he could hear Ol' Billy Joe et cetera chirping. "But, of course, if they show up for it, ain't no way we can expose our precious children to no psycho. And in this state, they got no union, so they're screwed! We can shuck 'em as nut cases, and if they get smart, we'll go public with it. The Press just loves it when a teacher goes loony tunes."

"Speaking of psycho," said Harmon Bullington, "I have discovered that the mere mention of Parent Involvement is good for a ten on the TSF scale! It is one of the major stressers, perhaps the worst one."

"Son, ah hear whut yer sayin'. Yuh kin stand afore a mob of teachers and say, 'We gotta encourage more Parent Involvement in the schools,' and it looks like a bunch of rats got loose in the auditorium. It's like you hosed 'em down with with gas and stood there with a match."

"Well, we did a little investigating at Hugh Stone High, and we found a curious continuum of truths."

"Speak English, Boy."

"Well, we found that students are children, technically, but also that the students *have* children, and *their parents* are children!"

"You mean you got 15-year-old girls with babies, and their own mothers are in their twenties and never had a chance to grow up? Hell, boy, we don't need investigatin' to git that. That's the natural product of what we're doin' here. What's yer point?"

"Well, I just feel that if we got some money and actually paid the kids to bring their parents to school for conferences, it would probably push the TSF to Level 12—and our scale only goes to ten!"

"That would take some green, Son. But we'll take a look

at it, and Ah'll put out the threatening bulletins to all the buildings right after the meetin'." He would spit about here—and miss some.

And then, like all the bulletins, it would arrive in the teachers' mailboxes.

Bulletin: Teachers who do not call parents on a regular basis will have Friday parent conferences from now on.

Bulletin: Teachers who do not stand by their doors will have extra parent conferences.

Bulletin: All teachers caught leaving campus early will get lunch duty for a week.

Bulletin: Teachers who do not hand in written modifications for the ever-growing legions of Special Ed. students mainstreamed to their classes will be denied bathroom privileges until graduation.

Bulletin: Teachers who are late with their lesson plans will hand out condoms in class every Friday until the end of the semester.

Bulletin: Teachers who do not get In-Serviced on "Spoon Feeding the Illiterate Freshman" will lose their rooms to office space and be re-assigned to broom closets.

"Always make the punishment fit the crime, Son—even if it don't make no sense. And, rule by threat!"

It had to be that way. Nothing as horrible as increased Parent Involvement could happen without serious organization. In the old days in the Corn Belt, Mr. Sherman had known many sane parents: well-adjusted adult parents. But times had changed, and he had moved into a city, and the goal of his profession had changed: Build Young Egos! To hell with skill and knowledge—Self Esteem is the product. Now a generation of parents had arrived that threw in with the kids in all situations, suspected the teacher, brought lawyers along, demanded things like Equity and Inclusion and "No Homework" and "No Competition." What was not needed was more of them coming to school. The terror of it made Mr. Sherman sweat again—even after all these years.

A woman came flying at Mr. Sherman's face. He was trying to focus on flakes of snow at the sliding glass door, and there she came. A swirling snowflake, then teeth, then the whole woman coming headfirst across the table at a parent conference.

"You sonovabitch!" she was screaming and flying right at his nose. Arms were reaching for her from both sides, but she was a missile, a projectile, red-eyed, sharp-toothed and foaming at the mouth!

He remembered her. She frequently came flying at him in these night sessions. She was part of the sleeplessness.

Like all parent meetings, it had been a volatile situation. Present were six teachers, one counselor, a vice principal, and an angelic child of sixteen. And, of course, the mother. As Mr. Sherman recalled, the child was explaining. "I'm a *&¢%$#@in' slut, a *&¢%$#@in' whore, a *&¢%$#@in' junkie, and a *&¢%$#@in' dealer, but I'm not a *&¢%$#@in' bitch! That's you, Mother Dear: you are the *&¢%$#@in' bitch!"

"See what I have to put up with? Such language!"

"It is the language she uses in class," a history teacher intoned.

"And I'm knocked-up because your *&¢%$#@in' boyfriend can't keep his *&¢%$#@in' hands offa me!"

"You shut your *&¢%$#@in' face, you little #%¢&, or I'll rip off your *&¢%$#@in' head and #$%¢& down our neck!"

"You know what I'm hearing here?" asked the counselor, "I'm hearing conflict. I sense tension between you two."

Mr. Sherman turned blue and nearly ducked under the table. It was politically incorrect to completely break up laughing at such conferences. He made sure his eyes never met another teacher's eyes—or it would have been all over, as the saying goes. He began the development of his hiatal hernia that day, trying to swallow that laugh.

"You bet your sweet @%#&* we got conflict, Bitch! But that's none of your *&¢%$#@in' business! I'm outa here," snapped the girl as she rose and made a quick feint toward the door.

"Wait a minute, Miss. We're not through," said the vice principal. And the security guard appeared at the door and turned the girl back.

"Now, you are failing all of your classes, and you have falsified exit papers and transferred yourself out of the school with forged documents, and you set off a fire alarm trying to escape. You are in trouble."

The girl sat down.

"Now, Madame, are you aware of these charges?"

"Oh, that. That's not the problem. A few papers, a little forgery. That's nothing."

"That's bad," said the counselor knowingly.

"That," said the mother, rising, "is nothing. It is not important, it is minor—it is creative—funny! It is no big deal. It is . . ."

"It's criminal," said Mr. Sherman. And the woman was unaccountably airborne. She had come flying right at his nose across that table, screaming "sonovabitch," arms flailing away, as teachers, counselor, vice principal, kid—everyone reached for her.

Mr. Sherman was ready for her, of course, and grabbed her and snapped her neck and tossed her aside like a rag doll. He wished. He could have it that way now if he wanted. He could fix that too.

Years had passed, however, and the incident was over—handled long ago. Gravity got the woman. She fell short and was subdued by other people. The angelic child had her baby in the county jail, and Mr. Sherman never found out what happened to the mother. But he now assumed that she had undergone a growth program to address her self-control situation. Still, her image could come flying at him almost anytime.

Mr. Sherman slammed his eyes shut and refused to let any more really bad parent conference images spoil any more of his evening. After all, this was one of the better ones. He had spoken only two words at the whole meeting. (Well, one of them was a contraction, but what the hell.) Such a reaction. Go figure!

At the sliding glass door now, Mr. Sherman watched the snow flurries. It was beginning with the "little Lux-like flakes" (from "Sixteen," by Daly, as he recalled). He picked out a flake and followed it to its destination, then went up and picked up another one, then another, tracing them down in their variant spirals long enough for eyestrain to overcome him. Or was he finally sinking toward sleep? The snow required watching. He was making it snow by paying close attention, being grateful, enjoying. Bliss. Peace. He considered waking his wife to take over for him—to watch and appreciate the snow, so that it would not quit. By dawn, school would be impossible; and so he stayed and did his duty.

He reached up with his eyes and found another snowflake and guided it in. Grabbed another and landed it. Gently lowered this flake and that. And soon they had faces, thousands of faces. He began to recognize individuals—kids—students from the 37 years—some from corn country, some from the suburbs, some from the ghetto—the smart ones, the dumb ones. Hell yes, there were dumb ones! Some kids are dumber than stumps! You just can't say so until you are retired. And some are magic and wonderful and pretty brilliant. And when they hit, softly, even his stomach felt better.

But, as usual, there were too many. He turned away, and there in the dark stood a full bird U.S. Marine Colonel. Here was a man who could really snap your neck, by God! He looked old and tough and mean—and weary.

"Mr. Sherman, I'm Jerome's father."

"Glad to meet you, sir. Welcome to Parent Night."

"You do at least know Jerome, Mr. Sherman?"

"I know him, sir. He sits right back there in that corner during Period 3. Yessir."

"Know right where he sits, huh?"

"Certainly."

"And have you spoken to him lately?"

"Well, I'm sure . . ."

"You have never spoken to him. Are you aware of that?"

"No, sir. I try to speak to everyone each class period. What do you mean?"

"I mean that boy idolizes you, and you haven't sat down and talked to him. Outside of speaking his name in roll call, you won't give him the time of day!"

"I . . . I . . ."

"He comes here hoping—and, God, knows, hope is about all he's got—doesn't have a fine mind or good study habits—just barely gets by. But you. You he likes—thinks you're special. And you don't talk to him."

"I have 180 students right now."

"I know what it's like to handle a lot of people, Mister. Don't give me that."

"But Jerome never causes trouble, never fights, never curses, never has seizures or panic attacks . . ."

"And you reward him by ignoring him?"

"Well, I . . ."

"He just sits there and rots because you won't talk to him. Do you ever call on him?"

"He never raises his hand."

"You couldn't call on him anyway?"

"Some parents say that damages the ego of the child who doesn't know the answer!"

"You never offer him any help, isn't that right?"

"He never asks for help. He is getting a C."

"And so you ignore him and let him sit back there like a piece of furniture. Did you know that he was A.D.D.?"

"Everybody is A.D.D."

"Here he is fighting that battle—takes Ritalin to get through the day—and you won't talk to him."

"I'm sorry."

"You sure as hell are."

"I will try to make contact tomorrow, and from now on. If he likes me, I like him."

"I don't think so, Mr. Sherman. I think we're talkin' transfer here. You have already ruined his young life—personally!" And, was that a tear in the corner of his eye?

The day after that one was Friday, and the Margarita bunch crept into the gloom of the little bar—more subdued than usual. It was always that way the day after Parent Night, but this was really gloomy!

Jerry was already there when Mr. Sherman arrived, and the chips and salsa were there somewhere in the dark. Mr. Sherman felt his way into his seat, and his Margarita appeared as if by magic, as usual. Wordless so far. Both men two-handed their drinks, lifting them like priests lift The Chalice.

"Had a visitor last night, Mr. Sherman," Jerry said, almost lightly, but with a dark dread hanging.

"We all did," Mr. Sherman growled.

"But mine was special," said Jerry. "Marine Colonel! Told me I had his boy in my class all semester and hadn't spoken to him—totally ignored him—ruined his life."

There was silence in the room. It reminded Mr. Sherman of the sixty seconds of silence the school observed when one of its pushers, a junior boy, was murdered in a deal gone sour. That was quiet.

"What!" said Jerry, sensing intrigue.

"And I'll bet you were that boy's favorite human being ever, right?"

"Naturally."

"You were the reason he was coming to school at all. That kid by-God idolized you, Jerry—thought you hung the moon! And you ignored his ass!"

"Were you listening at my door again?"

"Hell no! The Colonel came to my room and laid the same trip on me!"

"But *I* was his idol."

"Nope, *I* was."

"I heard the man say, and I believed him, that *I* was the kid's idol."

"As they say in Russia, Bolshevik! I was the idol. It was I—I, as in idol."

"Hell, let's drink to idleness, Mr. Sherman. It's Friday."

A faculty has a grapevine that is very efficient, and it became apparent in the following days that Jerome's teachers all had that same visit, almost word-for-word. Not Colleen, of course, because if Jerome had been her student, she would have had him face-to-face, convincing him that a square was really a rectangle, or some such thing. But Jerome had six teachers, and he apparently idolized them all; and after the colonel's night at Hugh Stone High, every one of them held Jerome's hand, spoon fed him, and took care of his needs, no matter what happened to the rest of the kids. Mr. Sherman guided him softly in for his landing, like a jittery snowflake.

Parents of kids with special needs are fighters, and they need to be in today's world. But there was a big fad on the loose at Hugh Stone High, and every kid that seemed to have any fire, every kid who had trouble sitting still, every kid who had a glint in his eye was dragged into the Special Ed. office and branded A.D.D.—as per Think Tank instructions, with pediatricians in the middle of the deal. The kids were pilled down and sent off into the melee. How could there suddenly be so many with this disorder? It looked fishy to everybody, but teachers are not equipped to diagnose such things. Someday, however, they will be blamed, unofficially, but on the record.

"Damn, that'll be a good Margarita meeting," Mr. Sherman mumbled. But then, when was there ever a bad Margarita meeting?

Now, with his Diet Coke in hand, he went back to the sliding glass door. Too many flakes now, coming from the West, horizontally, fast. There would be snow, all right, enough for a good plump cover.

And that, for Mr. Sherman, was an excuse to worry about all the things he wanted covered by time and forgetfulness and forgiving. Surely there were others that he had neglected along the way: kids he had failed to teach citizenship or patriotism or good manners; kids he had failed to warn about sexually transmitted disease or potentially dangerous traps; kids he had slighted because of paranoia or some current mania or phobia; guns or knives he had missed; thugs he had let win little victories; girls he had ogled unconsciously; negative ethnic thoughts he had harbored. He had doubtlessly snapped at people, shown temper.

But this was the night he was going to stay awake and come to some sort of resolution—perhaps forgive himself, or add it all up and honestly absolve himself. By morning! This was going to be the last night of this madness, dammit! It was time to let history fade back into history—where it belonged—re-write it if necessary, but get it into perspective.

"We gonna twist some of these teachers up so bad they'll just stay twisted the rest of their lives. The Seven Cardinal Principles demand it! Ah luv this job, Boy!" Bastard.

Somebody had to be up there turning the screws like that. This night had been in the works for a long time.

"My friend, I am sure there is no Think Tank," he remembered Jerry saying over a Margarita. "In fact, at times I think there is no thought, let alone a Think Tank. I am equally sure, however, that there are laws at work here. Patterns, maybe." He opened his hand, lifted it towards his face, and stroked downward on his mustache and beard.

"You're talking about chance."

"Nope. There's predictability involved. You see it enough times and you figure it out. Pop Quiz: How long does your average five-year plan last?"

"Two years."

"Right. And how do you know that?"

"Because I've seen a dozen of them and I've only been here twenty-five years."

"Question Two: What do you do if a gang of Arab terrorists invades the school, kills off the whole six-pack of cops, and takes all of us hostage?"

"I stand by my door."

"And why is that?"

"Because whatever goes wrong, whatever problem we have, it will be all right if we just stand by our doors!"

"Damn straight." A careful sip of Margarita here. Jerry liked his frozen; Mr. Sherman on the rocks. "Question Three: On every written form that comes from downtown, they have a racial code. You've got B for Black, W for White, H for Hispanic, O for Oriental, NA for Native American. And even though there hasn't been an Eskimo kiddo here in the deep South in my considerable lifetime, why does the form always include AN—for Alaskan Native?"

Now that was a tough one, but Mr. Sherman was up to it. In those days he read a little. Not much, but some. "They're starting a kayak team?"

"Ennnnggghhhh!" went Jerry, imitating the quiz show buzzer that said you blew it. And then Jerry would take a sip of his Margarita, slowly and dramatically. "I have it on the best of authority—from friends of friends who know important people—that the district has seven tons of *Walrus* in the warehouse, and they want to serve it in the cafeterias." It was probably true. "You need Eskimos."

Jerry understood the system, God help him. And Mr. Sherman missed Jerry—wanted to get him out here on this mountain, sit down with Margaritas, and hold a few truths to be self-evident.

"Ebb and flow—tides with the times—Natural Laws. But not a Think Tank. Most of this stuff bears none of the marks of actual thought," he would say.

"But that's cynical."

"Your Think Tank is cynical. My way has no villains."

"But your way is unexplained. And it has victims. My way has victims, but it has a place to put the blame. You can't fight mysterious laws and tides and coincidences. Having Ol' Billy Joe Jim Bob Willie Wayne Kline gives you something to strike back at!"

"Mr. Sherman, you have just ended a sentence with a preposition."

Friday afternoon was good for the soul.

Mr. Sherman shook off the attack of nostalgia with a fond toast with a hoisted Diet Coke to the fading image of his friend.

Outside it was getting Christmassy. How ironic that this snow should come in January, so far from Christmas. A puff of wind tossed a cloud of snow across the yard in the light of a large automatic yard light just outside the sliding glass door, and Mr. Sherman felt warm inside and out. He was okay: he was indoors and secure, and there was no school tomorrow. Surely this was the best of all possible worlds!

Right about then, however, out there in the snow, developing like a picture, he saw a set of tracks—parallel white lines in the darker dirt of the driveway. The light now sifted into the grooves, and the tracks came into relief before his eyes. And he knew where they came from—that's not the point. He knew that he had run a garden cart through the remains of a pile of topsoil he had just moved in the warm days preceding the storm. Now the frozen grooves were filling up with snow. Tracks.

He knew all of that, but Mr. Sherman was in the mood to overread things—like the five-day seminar he once did on one poem: "Kubla Khan." Beat that poor damn poem to death! And so the tracks became grocery cart tracks: Miss Whitby's stolen grocery cart. Soon he was seeing her image developing there, wandering with her stolen Safeway cart, searching—or maybe the replacement cart—searching, trying to find a room, somewhere to teach, to fulfill herself. It grew worse, and she was limping down there in the snow, the wind pounding her. Before long he was seeing himself down there at her side, trying to help her, mentoring! They were searching together, but there was no room.

No room at the inn. Mr. Sherman slapped himself. He had to crush this willed fantasy before that damned cart became the jackass, Miss Whitby the Virgin Mary, and himself Joseph! Joseph had failed Mary, technically, in coming up with a manger instead of a decent room, and Mr. Sherman had failed Miss Whitby. And that was a crock and he knew it! He had only been her mentor, not her principal. What could one mentor do against a thousand tormentors?

"All right, that's it. I've got the damn language out playing with it. That's counterproductive." Mr. Sherman grabbed a handfull of his hair and shook himself—gently, of course. He did not need to hear one of those "Karrack" sounds. But he did have to face the fact that, somewhere not so deep inside, he still thought he could have fixed Miss Whitby's situation if he had tried.

But he had tried. He had gone to the seminar.

He had gone to a thousand seminars and In-Service sessions over the years. Was that not trying? Very much so.

"Well," he admitted, looking around the shadowy room, "I did steal that other cart for her: the one from the Salvation Army Thrift Store." And Mr. Sherman cringed.

He caught sight of himself again in a reflection, and he cringed some more. His language had gone slangy, and that was bad enough, but his appearance had really deteriorated. Oh, he had never been a suit and tie sort—especially not in recent years when such costuming might intimidate or belittle someone, as well as bake his brains. But this image in the reflection was more than casual.

His outfit was stunning, probably the latest thing for the ups and downs of night life for the retired in winter: a sort of cranberry top of rugged fleece, a mango bottom, fleece also—elastic waist and ankles, and the little flat "Andy" cap of Harris tweed, "Hand Woven in the Outer Hebrides." He always cocked the little flat hat to one side. It went with everything, after all, having eight classic patterns of Tweed sewn together in one spectacular presentation. And then the serape on top of the fleece. No socks, of course. Socks would have him slipping around on the new hardwood floor he himself had nailed down. A terrible pain hit him. "With Wifey's help! *We* nailed down the floor!" The pain left.

And then his mind jumped again, and he wondered if Joseph ever stopped to ask directions. He would have to check.

He studied his reflection. "I like to think of this as the new sixty."

Chapter Four

Mr. Sherman wanted to do the right thing. Teachers in general want to do the right thing and are convinced, often with a great deal of coercion, that the newest thing is the right thing. Someone always makes sure there is a new thing before anybody knows whether anything has worked! American Public Education might have zoomed past the perfect thing twenty years ago and not noticed because everybody was excited about 30 other things. Damndest thing.

When a new "thing" came to the district, the Think Tank was always in the thick of the fray. Mr. Sherman tried the black window again and brought Ol' Billy Joe et cetera into focus.

"'Sears Ol' Shirley Knott," brayed Ol' Billy Joe. "Boy, you gonna luv her! She gonna make yer skin crawl, Boy! 'Specially if y'all think yer a By-God adult."

Harmon Bullington's introduction to Ol' Shirley Knott had to be a fateful moment. Combining her talents with those of Bullington was going to result in TSF's above and beyond the call of Horace Mann. It was goin' to be deep and wide: District wide and butt deep! And so, so annoying, moment to moment.

Ol' Shirley Knott was a tall woman, and not bad looking. It was her particular position in the scheme of things that made her so effective. Number One, she had put in several years at a grade school—to the point where she could not talk to an adult. She was liable to reach over and cut your meat for you at lunch, or wipe your nose or something. Number Two, her husband was a CEO in a mid-sized corporation. And so she brought a whole clip of magic bullets from private industry into education—with grade school rhetoric.

"Good morning, boys and gir . . . young people," she would say to a faculty group. "Today we are going to take an awesome journey. Can you say, 'Awesome Journey'?" And Harmon Bullington sat and etched into his diabolical soul the faces of the teachers. Mr. Sherman's face would have been a good place to start.

Bullington held up a card that read "9.7"—and Shirley Knott was pleased. The latest thing was coming down in a horrendous new In-Service session.

"Now, everybody join hands. Go ahead, take the hand of the teacher to the left of you and the teacher to the right of you..that's it. Oh, you are a good group of boys and . . . young teachers. Now, shut your eyes—shut 'em, really tight. Don't peek. Oh, I see somebody peeking! Naughty teacher! Okay, now, rock back and forth from side to side . . . and breathe . . . breathe in and breathe out . . ."

"Is there any other way? For crissakes, what is this?" Mr. Sherman peeked. A wave of nausea hit him—still hit him all these years afterward. It was beginning of the reign of Shirley Knott and her infernal In-Service training sessions. That first time, she was "giving" the teachers personal power, helping them discover themselves—find out who they really were. They did some terrible breathing that day, and a lot of really embarrassing things: monologues including personal secrets, weaknesses, phobias; confessions about embarrassment and mortification; god-awful, private, body-function stuff that was nobody else's business. They swung hands and patty-caked, sang songs and danced, and they hugged. At the end of it, they were supposed to feel "empowered"—whatever that was.

What it was was a three-Margarita meeting in the making. But the teachers, bless 'em, had gone along with it. In-Service training was part of the deal, and they had signed up for the whole deal. Mr. Sherman wanted to snap Shirley Knott's back with a loud "Karrack!"—but he didn't really want to touch her.

"That was really special, boys and g . . . young . . . . —really special. Can you say, 'Special'?" A scattered answer, maybe. "Now, don't you feel the power? Don't you feel just like walking into that classroom of yours and taking it to the next level?"

When you talk to an English teacher about taking it to the next level, he thinks of Dante and the many levels of Hell. And Mr. Sherman had an idea that he was in the front row on the worst level.

"Let's give each other a round of applause." And she would lead the patty-caking.

Later there would be leadership camp and team training, and Encounter—just Encounter. Sometimes they would play with blocks, and sometimes they would be the blocks others played with. They joined hands and tied Gordian knots with a dozen people; they walked logs, tightrope-style; they wove poly-rope webs and tried to pass 300 lb. colleagues through holes in the web without hitting the rope, they intentionally fell from great heights—backwards—and caught each other. They used all five of their senses on each other.

And when it was over, they split up into several color-coded groups, made up mindless lists, put it all down on butcher paper, and came together again, compiled a mighty list on a wall, and went away and forgot the whole thing. And Shirley Knott absolutely squirted! Ol' Billy Joe et cetera cackled. Harmon Bullington observed and wrote and got his Ph.D. And Mr. Sherman became ever more and more jaded.

And now he was standing by the sliding glass door, breathing in and breathing out, watching the snow entering the pool of light, streaking down out of the darkness. "My God," he thought, "I am standing by my door."

"All right, Son, we gonna toss some figgers around here. Press'll believe just about anythin' we tell 'em, if it sounds like some sorta confession—meanin' we can pitch out negative crap about ourselves and they'll eat it up. Then we sorta point 'em to all the right conclusions.

"'Sears a buncha data I cobbled up last night when I was up with indigestion and gas. How 'bout 65% of our kids admit to bein' on hard dope, 91% of 'em have done booze, over half of 'em's sexually active, and say 20% got homosexual tendencies. Y'all kin mix 'em up if yuh want to—thing is, they all bad!"

"But how about the TSF's?"

"Yer just new, Son. Y'all gonna git caught up. Lissen: We lay all that on 'em, and we stick in there the idea that 11% of the kids are absent from school on the average day. Whose fault is that?"

"The teachers?"

"Now you thinkin' with me, Son! And so whose fault is all this dope and sex and twisted crap?"

"Gee, Professor, I guess that would be the teachers, too!"

"Hell yes! Plain as the nose on yore face."

"You Rock, Sir."

"That's Doctor Sir, Son." (That would be back before he became Doctor Son.) "See, we git The Press to see that the kids are stayin' out of school and gettin' into dope and booze and sex because the teachers cain't teach! That's yer TSF connection. None of 'em smart enough to turn it around and see they gettin' in trouble 'cuz they just naturally rotten li'l som'bitches in the first place." Big ol' ugly brown splotch of reeking juice about here.

"I could come up with an In-Service about 'How to Attract Murdering, Thieving Little Perverted Druggie Sex Fiends to YOUR Classroom,'" offered Shirley Knott.

"We'll have a two-hour test . . ." said Dr. Minnie Mae Lizbutt.

"Work on it, Gals. Sounds like a plan to me. But I got more here. We gonna hit this on all levels. We gonna require that ever school call all them kids' homes, chase all them kids down, drag 'em back to the school, and throw 'em back into class. Require teachers to catch 'em up! We gonna pick 'em up at home, drag 'em to school in the morning, feed 'em breakfast, escort 'em to class, and make the teachers guard 'em all day. If one escapes, we on him like a pack o' hounds, catch him agin', and drag his butt back to class!"

"That should disrupt everything all day long!"

"Don't y'all jist luv it! Then, git this: we gonna make sure ever teacher gets chewed out personally fer not teachin' *Responsibility!*"

Even though Harmon Bullington was new at that phase of the operation, he had to admit that the plan had depth. Ol' Billy Joe et cetera was a master.

"We gonna git some percentages outa this, too: say . . . uh . . . 36% of teachers missed a certain number of absences—or 62% of kids cut class to have sex in the bathroom and just left the building afterwards . . . get the security people pissed off, too. Hell, we jist blame the computers fer all the numbers, like with elections."

The more pragmatic people in the school buildings

watered down some of it, of course. It would have been impossible to work in the school and hand down every outrage that came down the pipe. Someone would have been hurt. Administrators, like principals and vice principals, had to live in the real world. "Poor bastards," thought Mr. Sherman. "Wonder where they drank their Margaritas?"

But he could not conjure up their faces. The details were fading. No animosity, apparently. Mr. Sherman could barely hear the imagined voices of the Think Tank. He was safe now, standing by his door in the snowy night all these years later. The features of the immediate landscape were fading also with the modest build-up of snow. By morning, all would be transformed; the details would be buried. It seemed late, and, in spite of the Diet Coke, Mr. Sherman felt another attack of drowsiness. He slid the glass door aside and got a face-full of fresh snow.

He remembered what a cold slap in the face it was when he sat down and summed up the "contributions" of the alleged Think Tank. Someone had to be in charge of things like paying students to come to school (with T-shirts, money, trophies, etc.); somebody had to dream up the Teacher Competency Test, which, if you passed it, certified you as literate for five years (and no longer); someone had to be deliberately pitting the fire department and the EPA against the school system, with sets of conflicting rules and schedules; someone from Hell was on board down there preaching Conformity and rewarding the big mavericks, making teachers feel guilty about their creativity because it flies in the face of the almighty "Consistency"; all of them had to be getting a great kick out of mocking the instincts of nurturing and fairness in teachers; someone had to be in charge of linking everything to government money, retirement funds, merit pay, or grant money.

Mr. Sherman tried to imagine what they would drink down there. Margaritas were out: only the good guys would drink Margaritas. No, it would be something vile. Buttermilk, probably. Buttermilk could turn Mr. Sherman inside out: could make him reach way back inside his very being and hurl forth all the poisons from the remotest corners of each cell: violently, immediately. They just had to be drinking buttermilk down there.

In the movie, Rip Torn would play Ol' Billy Joe et cetera. The accent would be better: not a pure diphthong anywhere. "Ah cain't honor stain yawl!"—with a lisp on the S. And as for Dr. Minnie Mae, well, you would probably get Al Franken all together in drag and dark-rimmed glasses out of the fifties—with chains, of course. Shirley Knott would be Whoopie Goldberg or Sigourney Weaver, depending on the director: beauty, sexuality, and danger. William H. Macy would play Harmon Bullington, mainly because you can't make a movie without William H. Macy ever again. It's the grin. Yeah. That bunch, with buttermilk!

Out on the highway, an eighteen wheeler roared through, pushing a pile of air and a cloud of snow. The roads were still open, but then, with any luck, this storm was just beginning. And then, a bus! Certainly not a tourist bus, the usual fare on this highway. You don't take tourists out into a good snowstorm. But it was definitely a bus. And it "transported" Mr. Sherman.

The big experiment with the city bus system crashed into his mind, and he said, "Why not?" And so he called it up and played it through: *City Buses Collide With School District!*

"Free Bus Service for One Full Day" was the good news advertised by the city's bus line. The bad news was that this wonderful promotional exercise would happen on a Wednesday. Wednesday was a school day.

The "thinking" was that people would ride the bus to work and discover that it was not a bad way to get to work. It would get a lot of cars off the road, and it would make the city bus system more popular and lucrative. To the kids, however, it was a miracle! So they hopped off the school bus as it arrived and hopped on a nearby city bus, and were gone. Downtown, the mall, whatever.

By noon it was on TV: three hundred school kids had congregated on one downtown street corner.

Credit the governor: it was decided early not to scramble the National Guard; but the situation was a definite SWAT call-up! Gangs of cops with menacing weaponry, tear gas, dogs, and hard-shelled vehicles descended upon the corner from every angle. Here a bus, there a bus, everywhere a cop bus . . .

And they loaded all those kids up and took them to safe areas—their schools, where 2500 at a time were routinely impounded on one city block, "contained" by unarmed teachers. Society was made safe again by early afternoon. Order was restored. On the six o'clock news, terrorized downtowners wept over the horror of it all. "They were everywhere . . . it wasn't safe . . ."

Fortunately, the city had laws about how many kids could be in one place at one time. Safety, after all, was the issue.

The following year, the city bus line used another strategy, probably fearing that teachers would grab those seats and head for downtown, or the mall, or maybe an early Margarita.

"I don't know," said one parent on TV, "I take the kid to school, let him off outside the building, and they can't get him to class? What are we paying these people for?"

Mr. Sherman pulled a chair over by the sliding glass door and sat down. He decided that if six feet of snow fell, he was going to watch it all. Twenty-seven years he had lived in that huge city where winter was one cold Tuesday afternoon in February—brown and gray. This was not going to be Minnesota, but it was going to be cold and snowy for a while, and very satisfying. The trees would re-cycle; the ticks would freeze; Bambi and Thumper would get furry. Jimminy Cricket would have to come by the hearth . . . But Mr. Sherman would stay awake. Alert. Figure it all out. Awake.

"Harm, my boy, y'all really opened up a can o' worms with this attendance thing. If we can blame the teachers for absenteeism, we can count that right into their assessments."

"You sonovabitch!" Woman, flying right at his nose!

"You will be her mentor . . ."

Mr. Sherman's lids became heavy. Very heavy. Very very . . .

"Spotted Liver to Bird Dog One. Spotted Liver to Bird Dog One. Come in. What's your twenty? Over."

"Uh . . . Spotted Liver, this is Bird Dog One. I'm at the rolling fist fight in the Gagateria Annex. Over."

"Uh . . . copy, Bird Dog One, but that can't be. I am at the rolling fist fight in the Gagateria Annex, and I do not have you in sight. Repeat: I do not have you in sight. Over."

"Uh . . . Spotted Liver, I copy that. I do not have you in sight either. Are you down, Spotted Liver? Over."

"Negatory, Bird Dog One. I am vertical—repeat: vertical. %@#*! Damn! Uh . . . correction, Bird Dog One . . . I am down. Repeat: I am down. Over."

"Uh . . . copy, Spotted Liver. Are you at the bottom of the pile at the East Entrance? Over."

"That's Affirmative, Bird Dog One: East Entrance, flat on my *&¢$#%$in' back. Over."

"Well, get your *&¢$#in' elbow out of my ribs! That's me on the floor with you! Over and Out!"

All the cops and the vice principals at Hugh Stone High

carried Walkie-Talkies when it was in fashion, and sometimes they were in over their heads anyway. The bell would ring, and it was like throwing a stick into an ant hill: 2400 kids would squirt into the halls to fight, kiss, snack, kill, run, scream, or just swim from Point A to Point B—in one piece, if possible. The radio traffic was sometimes frantic.

"Uh . . . Eager Beaver, this is Bird Dog Two. We've got two men down in the Gagateria Annex. Let's bail 'em out."

A little cold Diet Coke in his lap woke Mr. Sherman up in a hurry. This was going to be tougher than he thought. The snowfall was hypnotic. He would have to keep his mind engaged—with those old demons. He willfully called up Ol' Minnie Mae Lizbutt . .

"This year I have already set up 32 days of testing," she was bragging. "We have the SAT, TAAS, ITED, RBI, COD, PDQ—Entry tests, Exit tests, psychological tests, diagnostic tests, Local, State, and National tests. Give me some time to think and I'll eliminate teaching altogether. We'll just test all day, every day."

"Now now, Dr. Minnie Mae Lizzbutt Honey, let's not jist go hog wild here. We'll drive 'em all out and won't have nobody to torment. Cain't y'all just pause a little and do somethin' with the scores?"

"Gotcha covered! As usual, we'll have the computers manufacture some numbers, and we'll leak the results to The Press before they're officially announced—so that they'll have time to line up some low blows at the staff! And we'll compare 'em to results from back before we screwed up the system. And, of course, blame the teachers."

"I can hear 'em now: 'But that's comparing apples and oranges! Ynah ynah ynah!'"

"And we can put 'em along side private school results. That'll piss 'em off."

"Funniest thing: ever notice that the public admires them private schools that make the kids wear uniforms, toe the line, behave like humans, do homework, come to school, respect their elders and all that bullshit? Then the minute you try any of that in the public school, they march in the streets with misspelled signs and demand mediocrity! We can work with that! First thing you know, they'll want to have PRIVATE public schools!"

"Yeah. We'll have schools of three or four hundred kids. Won't be fun anymore."

For a moment there, it almost sounded like there was some shred of decency in one of those two. Mr. Sherman got to his feet. "I've got to keep things straight. I'm half asleep here. These people probably burn butterflies, sell kiddie porn—or worse. We can't have any bleed from the moral sector."

"Tell yuh what we'll do, Doctor Minnie Mae Honey, you git yer 32 days of tests, and we'll have a big ol' In-Service about Time Management—and kick the teachers' asses for not teachin' more and testin' less. Tell 'em the computers said so. Git maximum TSFs there."

That was more like it. Mr. Sherman poured up some Diet Coke to replace the spilled stuff. He hated to drink alone, but what the hell.

"Wait a minute. In my fantasies, I don't drink alone!" He made the correction, easily, swiftly.

The Bearded One gave his frozen Margarita one small circular dip of the swizzle stick and put on his most enigmatic look.

"What?" questioned Mr. Sherman. Jerry was onto something. He never came right out with it, but he was working on some small intrigue.

"Look at Darby," he muttered, low profile.

And then it was obvious. Jerry had picked up on the joy, the muted exuberance of Darby McTrain. Her eyes, her posture, her whole demeanor was glowing. Naturally, she hadn't spoken. She wanted to have it dragged out of her. It was that good.

"What have you done, Train Person?" asked Mr. Sherman.

"Everything," she said. And then she released a huge grin that had joy and mischief in it, and deep satisfaction.

"Give," said The Bearded One. "It is Friday afternoon, and the meeting is convened."

"I had quite a week," she said brightly. "Well, Monday was not much, but on Tuesday I noticed that the doors to the classrooms in the new wing open *inward.* The Fire Marshal will pop a vein!"

"Did you report that?" asked Jerry.

"To the vice prince, the prince, the 'Board, the Fire Chief—hell, I put it on the Internet. If we are going to have rules, we are all going to have rules!"

Mr. Sherman knew the history. One day Darby McTrain had abandoned her post at her door and gone recklessly off to the restroom—one of those girl things, years ago. And she had been caught by a particularly narrow-minded vice principal whom she had since driven away. Now the rules were for all—and that meant all rules for all personnel. And if anyone had forgotten a rule, Train Person would remind him.

"Well done," said Jerry, lifting his glass. The deed was toasted all around. Only the four of them were at the meeting so far, but Colleen's smile, Darby's satisfied and devilish grin, and Jerry's bearded wisdom made it all an indelible moment for Mr. Sherman.

"But that isn't all," said Darby. "We had Wednesday, Thursday, and Friday!" All focused on Darby as she took a slow sip of her soda, relishing the moment. "On Wednesday, I counted the kids in the cafeteria during third lunch!"

"My God," said Mr. Sherman. "You counted them? All of them?"

"Yup. And there were too many!"

"Well, of course, too many. It's always a nightmare."

"But over a hundred too many! And that means mathematically that someone is not following the rules. Fire Code for one. We only have four lunch periods anyway because there are too many kids and too small a cafeteria. Almost one-third of our kids were there! That means someone is sending kids to more than one lunch. The Fire Marshal won't like it, and the principal won't like it."

"Uh . . . both have been informed, I assume," said Jerry.

"In writing. Twice. It's going to be beautiful."

"I say we shut the whole place down," offered Colleen.

"I'll drink to that."

"Wait! Thusday came along."

"I remember Thursday as if it were yesterday," said Mr. Sherman. Mr. Sherman's Margarita was very potent that day, probably.

"Thursday I was having a big test."

"Let me guess," said Colleen. "You caught a cheater."

"Worse. I caught a kid praying. Praying in school."

"Get out the tar and feathers!" said Jerry.

"You told the principal, of course—in writing?"

"I had to. It was her daughter!"

Ah, the joy of it! One of the great Fridays. They would pay and pay for crossing Darby McTrain.

"I read somewhere that we cannot pray in school. Federal law or something. We might offend someone who doesn't believe in God. Of course, next to her was a kid that I earlier heard cuss a blue streak—used language that would peel the paint right off a car! But I was told long ago that stuff like that was a cultural matter and not to bother with it."

"Well," said Jerry, "I sense that there is more."

"Oh, yes! Did anyone notice that Channel One was not on today? No kid-oriented news, no kid reporters, no kid-targeted commercials in school today?? I sense breach of contract here. They paid for access to the kids, and we went for it, and today someone didn't follow the rules."

"I say we shut the whole place down," repeated Colleen.

"Here's to shutting the whole place down!" A toast.

A Warm feeling came over the group, as usual. Life was good. It was what Friday was all about. Nobody else was bothered by any of this, of course, but Darby had a definite function. Someone had to fire back at The Bastards, and the Train Person had blasted away that week.

Later in the meeting, as Mr. Sherman remembered, it was learned that Colleen had been tutoring during her 30 minute lunch period when it became evident that the boy she was tutoring was unhappy. She bought him lunch, then she drilled him on his math. After school, she drove him home, met his single mom, bought him a pair of designer sneakers, got his mom a better job, set him up with an NFL lineman as a Big Brother, hooked him up with a church, got him to quit smoking and join AA, and removed a thorn from his paw. Okay, so maybe he over-remembered things a little. But that was Colleen all over. She saved them one at a time.

And Mr. Sherman had always worried about Colleen, because in that city, in that school district, as in many, no good deed went unpunished. He had known one lady who had given percentage points to students who gave blood at the school blood drive—and ended up national news because of it. Some students, after all, had no blood and could not win points, and so it was unfair. He knew a man who was jailed for being in his classroom working late at night. School was out for the day, after all, and he was supposed to go home. Saving the world from kids who prayed before tests was virtuous, so Darby was safe. But butting in, as Colleen routinely did, and helping a kid up from the bottom? That could be risky. Something could have been done to her for that. Fortunately, she slipped past The Bastards. At last report, she had just returned from Ireland. Again.

Mr. Sherman had slipped through, too—through all of it: no ruin, no infamy, perhaps no justice! He was thinking now of all of the bad things he had done, and the fact that he had never been run to ground, found out, punished. He had been a pragmatist in a world of Progressive Education. He could have been assassinated at any time. He was wired to take his "just desserts" right out of the atmosphere, however—the abuse that was wafted out there for all teachers—to get his bloody stripes whenever all teachers were whipped together. And there was plenty of that going on. Whenever someone wrote a book about bad teachers, or asked in an editorial what was wrong with schools—whenever a teacher was caught using or abusing a kid, Mr. Sherman took a hit.

It was only 1 A.M., unheralded by the Regulator clock with the screwed-up hands, and Mr. Sherman took a hit on his Diet Coke. He longed for order, logic.

"If not my Think Tank, who? With all the well-meaning teachers and administrators, and supposedly parents and politicians, why can't we do *Education*? And, if we can, why don't we? Nope. There is a force: my Think Tank! I rest my case." And he drank to his wisdom.

Chapter Five

The blank TV screen now arrested Mr. Sherman's attention. He had been watching too much TV lately, but then he always had. It was no substitute for an inner life, but it was not the wasteland people had worried about. It was a curiosity to him that on his many forays into the middle of the night he had found himself looking at the blank TV screen. There was something noble about how that screen kept on giving, even after the set was turned off. He saw his feet reflected there, and then he backed away and saw his legs—his former legs, his retired legs, his legs emeritus, the late great legs. And then Willard Scott.

And Willard introduced a picture of a 104-year-old lady auto mechanic who went to work every day on a Moped and drank beer with boys after work. Then there was another 104-year-old lady who had taught school for 80 years. And another who had actually read *The Scarlet Letter.* (Mr. Sherman had tried eight times—had taught the book twice in American Lit. classes!—but had never been able to get through that great book because it bored the hell out of him.) (You can't say that until you're retired.)

Then the screen turned yellow and black. Waves of guilt swept over Mr. Sherman, of course: any English teacher worthy of the name would be embarrassed to admit to using *Cliffs Notes.* "Aaaarrrrrrgggggghh!" (That's the way Schulz had the "Peanuts" kids scream.) He had done the same with *Moby Dick*: taught English 37 years and never read *Moby Dick* all the way through. Page upon page of the private lives of sperm whales would be knocked off in a minute by good old Cliff. And now there were actually *Cliffs Notes* on how to retire. All of this he had gotten away with until now. But he had read all of Steinbeck, dammit. So there!

He had shown the Gregory Peck *Moby Dick* to the kids in class after they had read excerpts of the book. And then there was feedback. Feedback was popular back then. But one kid had written a paper called, "A Ship Called the Pequod, A Dick Called Moby"—and Mr. Sherman had given it an A! "Aaaarrrrrrgggggghh!" Good paper, though.

But so "unprofessional," he thought. There was no point in coming out of hiding—going to a Cliffs Anonymous meeting or whatever. He had done it. It was one of the many things he had done to survive.

He stepped back and eyed the TV screen again. Willard and all the wonderful old ladies were gone, and the antique people were on, appraising things. They were working on an object he thought he recognized.

"What have you brought us, Madam?"

"It's a crystal apple, but the patina's shot to hell and I don't think it's signed."

The appraiser looked the object over and held it up to the light. "Aha. Here, floating inside, is an inscription: 'Presented to Mr. Sherman, Mentor, for the fine work with Miss Whitby.' Interesting."

"Well?" said the lady.

"Well what?" said the appraiser.

"What is it worth at auction?"

"I should think it would fetch about $5.35—on a good day, if the patina were not destroyed. In this condition, it is quite worthless."

Mr. Sherman sank to the couch. He was more sleepy than he had thought. But this was to be the night of slaying personal dragons, and he popped open his eyes as wide as possible.

"Mr. Sherman, how would you like to be visited by three or four ghosts and dragged through a night of hell, damnation, and finally redemption!"

Mr. Sherman sat up. Fast.

"Who said that?"

"How about it? Game?"

"Hell no. Who are you?"

"Who do I look like?"

Mr. Sherman looked at the figure in his recliner, somewhat illuminated by the ambient light from the yard light coming through the sliding glass door. "You look like Shakespeare—and my friend Jerry, mostly. But your outfit makes you look a little heavy."

"No need to insult your phantom shrink, Mr. Sherman. I have come to psychoanalyze you. The HMO sent me." The spectre consulted a 3x5 note card. "They have instructed me to say, 'This won't hurt a bit.'"

Mr. Sherman straightened and rubbed his eyes. It was still there. In his recliner, quite at home. "You won't tell anybody about this, will you?"

"I have to submit a report, in triplicate—one copy to the secretary of each entity that can hurt you most. And the secretaries will run off copies for their friends—and yours. It will be funny." He squirmed as if his tights were twisted.

"But I could lose my job for this!"

"You don't have a job, Ace. You are worthless, remember? You are retired. The thousands of lives you touched have gone on without you. You are no longer relevant. So hold still and take it like a man. If you are no longer a man, they have Viagra now."

"Leave Velma out of this!"

"Hmmmmm," said the shadowy figure. "Who is Velma—or, more accurately, who *was* Velma?"

"She is no one," said Mr. Sherman. It was snowing outside, but he was sweating again.

"But she was someone," chided the stranger.

"No, she was no one—she was just a kid: a kid who almost got me into trouble."

"Pardon me while I write down some cryptic remarks in my handy-dandy notebook," said the shrink. And he did, too.

Mr. Sherman protested. "Don't you write any of this down, dammit. I didn't hug her back!"

"Did you hug her front?"

"I did not. I didn't hug any of her. She was a kid, and I was 50 years old!"

"Still . . ."

"Still nothing. I didn't lay a glove on that girl!"

"Ah. Girl now. You didn't want to?"

Mr. Sherman searched very quickly for words. He ran through his entire vocabulary, which was considerable, and he mentally pushed some buttons on a small thesaurus device—solar batteries—and all that—that he sometimes used, like *Cliffs Notes*. But there were no words.

Finally, "I did not hug that girl."

"And you didn't want to."

More silence. "Come on, Sherm, goddammitt, you can do this." Only Mr. Sherman could call him Sherm. And maybe Velma.

He looked straight at the stranger, pointed his finger at

him, and looked him right in the eye, and said with all the force and sincerity he could muster, “I did not have hugs with that woman!”

And it sounded awfully familiar, somehow.

“No part of you wanted to hug that . . . woman, I believe you called her?”

“Nope. Not me. No way. Get out of my house! Who the bloody hell invited you, anyway?” Mr. Sherman came off the couch and made an excellent feint toward the recliner. But the shrink was gone. But whither?

“Into the air, and what seem’d corporal melted as breath into the wind . . .” Mr. Sherman had taught too much *Macbeth* and had been hugged once too often.

Over to the sliding glass door now. Back to landing snowflakes, trembling. But there was accumulation now. Familiar yard objects were beginning to transmogrify. Reality was slipping away outside, too. He had been asleep temporarily. No other explanation was acceptable. Unless this thing was getting away from him.

“Methinks thy story stinketh,” a voice hissed from the dark direction of the recliner. All the Jerry had gone out of the voice, and an Elizabethan sound, straight out of a pirated PBS video tape, assailed Mr. Sherman.

“Avaunt! and quit my sight!” he screamed. “Let the earth hide thee! Thy bones are marrowless, thy blood is cold!”

“But thy blood, Mister, was hardly cold! Nay, say rather it boiled! Deny it not!”

“Oh, full of scorpions is my mind..!”

“’Twas not thy scorpion that throbbed, but thy . . .”

“Thou canst not say I did it! Never shake thy gory looks at me!”

"There is nothing gory about my locks."

And then Mr. Sherman noticed something terrible. It was not a really good Shakespeare that he was seeing, it was the bust: the thing in the church at Stratford—the phony thing that did not look natural or human. It was the thing that simply could not have written the plays.

"False face must hide what the false heart doth know, right? That isn't really you there, is it?—and it never was! You never writ, and no man ever loved."

"Oh, lighten up, Mr. Sherman," the shrink said. "This English teacher crap doesn't have to be this heavy. Cripes!" And now he looked like someone else completely, and a little like himself. "Look, you got away with it. Enjoy."

Friend? Fraud? Freud? Mr. Sherman gave up—just quietly, there, alone in his living room—gave up a little. "All right, dammit, I admit it: the hugging was . . . nice. I liked it. There."

"Dost thou know thy guilt be madness?"

"You're not him. Edward De Vere, that was him. He. The Earl of Oxford wrote the plays. Don't be so damned smug!" The image was better now. The characteristics of the bogus bust softened. It was like shifting one's attention from an icon in a Central American church to one in a Protestant church: a less garish, more human face emerged. And Mr. Sherman softened his stance, too.

"I suppose, if I am going to get anything out of this, I had better just say this: Although I really did not hug her, she did hug me. Several times. Just walked up to me—repeatedly—on consecutive days, actually—and hugged. She pressed her . . . uh..self—top part, right into me, as it were . . ."

"Hmmmmm," and Will was at work with his quill, dashing off rapid notes.

Mr. Sherman went back to the couch. "What the hell," he said. "She pressed those . . . she pressed against me—on consecutive days, actually—and I was at least temporarily..uh..stimulated, I suppose. Mildly excited."

"There, now, Prufrock, was that so bad?" And then the shrink changed again. New elements were sifting into the image, accumulating, rather rapidly. "Damn, Boy! We gonna hunt you down like a dawg! We gonna posthumously kick yo' ass!"

And with that Mr. Sherman was awake for real. He had known about the girl, but he had never thought of himself as an Oxfordian! With English teachers, that can hurt! This was getting to be quite a night.

It was getting good outside, too. A blinding snowstorm it was not, but snowing it was, and happy was Mr. Sherman. (He had been fascinated with sentences in which the subjective complement was front-shifted and preceded the linking verb. But English teachers are subject to all sorts of madness.) An old Singer sewing machine his wife had turned into a planter now looked more like some kind of cart heaped with .... No! He stopped the grocery cart image in its tracks. He willed it away with his superior mind. No damned pile of snow was going to put Miss Whitby into his mind again. He had turned that whole thing into victory earlier on. (Just earlier would have sufficed.) Tomorrow she would arrive at her computer and boot it up at 9 A.M. like a real person. Somewhere around mid-morning she would have a coffee break—perhaps take an hour for lunch! Outside the racket, people lived like that. At five, after squinting at that screen all day, she would pull the plug on the damned thing and go home. And she would never know what it was like to feel a classroom full of kids gradually comprehend the madness of the duke in "My Last Duchess" or stop with Frost on a snowy evening and watch the woods fill up with snow. She would have coffee breaks and get to go to the john when she needed to. And nobody would need her, or just the image of her, just to get through the day. She would touch keyboards, not humanity. She would change nobody, perhaps nothing. And her eyes would turn into slots. He willed the whole image of her away with his superior mind. So there.

He looked out into the snow.

"You're dealing with an educated man here, dammit! I am through being manipulated."

God it was late. Mr. Sherman remembered a line from Mark Twain somewhere: "It smelled late." That would have to be footnoted if it appeared in a pile of research papers, but this was just between him and the sliding glass door. There was a wind now. The snow was deciding where to accumulate. There was going to be a nice drift by the garage, apparently, right at the crest of the rise out back. And by the pick-up in the driveway.

On the wall of the garage, a trellis was becoming a work of art, fraught with symbolism, inspiring thought, memories . .

Assessment Day for Mr. Sherman. He was ready for them. He had cobbled up a list of ELO's (Essential Learner Outcomes) that hit all the seven Cardinal Principles, and his lesson plans were immaculate for weeks past and into the future: all the bells and whistles, buzz words and jargon, phonied-up reams of total, but quality, bull! He even had his "modifications" for the five or six ADHD kids, the squad of left-handers, the hearing-impaired girl, the Russian boy, etc. Word in the lounge was that the era of "Teacher as Coach" was waning, and the assessors were now going for costumes: the "Broadway" approach. ("Teacher as Facilitator" was a year away at that moment.)

And so it was that, for his greatest dog & pony show ever, Mr. Sherman entered dressed as an Italian Renaissance duke. A boy in drag was hanging from a map hook right under the clock, and a girl from Cameroon, dressed as a monk, was painting him—with a 4" paint brush. The Russian kid played the dog (a wolf hound), and the ADHD kid played the pony. The dog had the bell and the pony had the whistle.

Never mind that there is no dog or pony, no bell or whistle in the dramatic monologue, "My Last Duchess," by Robert Browning. No, it's a poem in which a mad and arrogant duke (Mr. Sherman) sends a warning to his *next* duchess that his *last* duchess has made mistakes that have caused her to become a mere painting on his wall. Dead, you know. Pity, actually. Fra Pandolf, the monk, has painted the portrait, and the duke is "taking us through" the piece, revealing his little quirks and sending a most chilling message to all who would seek his fortune.

Never mind all that. This was show biz.

And it was a smash with the assessor! The "portrait" looked flirty, the "monk" painted furiously, the dog barked, the pony pooped, and Mr. Sherman was most menacing! Certain "plants" in the room asked rehearsed questions; others gave penetrating answers; less talented kids nodded knowingly and took "notes"—fully engaged. At one point, color-coded groups scampered everywhere. It was a blowout. Mr. Sherman got a 98.2 or a IV, or a "Superior"—whichever was simply top drawer at the time. A triumph. This was teaching!

He had actually done that, and attrocities similar to that, for many assessments, and he had done some real teaching when real teaching was in fashion—always trying to keep up with the game, trying to pick up through the faculty grapevine exactly what "good teaching" was on any particular day, and then, "leaping into ladies' laps and licking fingers." (*Cyrano,* probably.) Was symposium good today? Was "techy" the current rage? Group work? Emerging leadership? Would the character teacher win? The father figure? Hitler? Hold up the hoop and he would jump.

Integrity? Couldn't afford it. That was something for the one or two year crowd. The long-termers had to dance to the music played (at least while their door was open) to have staying power. Otherwise, private industry was still out there.

Nobody seemed to know what a school was, much less what a good teacher was. In Texas, someone would compare it to a refinery or pipeline: crude in one end, high octane out the other. In Oregon, it was a forest, perhaps—without a spot on any owl around! It would be like a wheat field in Kansas. Mr. Sherman thought about "hot dish" back home in Minnesota.

Hugh Stone High went for sort of a flavor-of-the-year approach to the multiple analogy routine.

Indeed, some years the school was a corporation, with stockholders out there needing to be pleased. Some years the school was a village: the village that reared the child. Some years it was the garden, covered deep in fertilizer, of course. Sometimes it was a great ocean liner, tossed upon choppy seas, but crossing the old pond with all hands on deck. Each of these constructs was meat for an in-service session, and target practice by Mr. Deeton, one of Mr. Sherman's favorite people, who held The Bastards responsible for everything.

"Well, what am I today?" he would say to the principal. "A vice president? The village blacksmith? A manure spreader? A deck hand? A galley slave? A facilitator, coach, punching bag? Or is it today that I am once again a teacher?"

"Gadfly, Mr. Deeton. Today and ever," was the usual response.

Mr. Sherman smiled now as he remembered a Shirley Knott visit to old Hugh Stone High, after classes were over, when most, but not all, were too weak to fight.

"Good afternoon, boys and gr . . . young teach . . . uh . . . Good afternoon everybody. Today's awesome journey is called, 'Our Factory.' Can you say 'Factory'?"

Nobody could even think it. But Dr. Knott had brought a whiz-bang chart to the session, and she wore a hard hat. Near the front of the faculty group, Mr. Deeton crouched, ready to spring, dangerous now, a 40-year veteran.

"Notice that in the middle, we have a big rectangle. It represents the factory—or school."

"We're a factory now," muttered Deeton. "I can't stand it."

"On the left, we have the raw materials, and all these little conveyor belts!" Many were still awake and grading papers at this point. The chart was projected on a large screen, and the art was clean. Shirley Knott added a little whistle to the top of the factory rectangle.

"Now, moving along these little conveyor belts into the factory are the paper, the pencils and pens, the stoooodents . . ." (She loved to drag out the word and stomp on the consonants at the end. She made broad sweeps with her arms—pumping motions—trying to get some enthusiasm going.) "And money, too. Can you say, 'Money'?"

And she showed the faculty how it was all supposed to work, according to the industrial paradigm. You simply fed in the money, paper, pens and pencils, kids, and incidentals like food, clothing, shelter, blood, sweat, and tears at one end of the rectangle, and you went to the other end and waited for the finished products to roll off the assembly line. You could build cars that way, TV sets, blenders, chain saws. So why not graduates? The more raw materials you put in, the more products you get out: a simple operation. Any questions?

Deeton pounced. "What about quality control at the supply end? What about quality control at the other end? Where is the conveyor belt for drugs? Alcohol? Weapons? TV? MTV? Family Dysfunction? Hormones? Diverse Cultures? Babies?"

Dr. Knott simply went on with her program and pointed to a conveyor belt leading into the factory from another rectangle. "This is the university, and this little belt feeds teachers into the factory: the assembly line's workers! You are our little factory workers."

"And so," said Mr. Deeton, "Some of us add bolts, some of us add nuts, some of us spray on a coat of paint, some of us solder in some circuitry—stick on a few labels?"

"Exactly!"

"Uh . . . when we paint 'em," said one of the black teachers, "are we changing their color?"

"Well . . ."

"Seems to me if you put a coat of paint on something, you change its color."

"Well, not necessarily . . ."

"Invisible paint, then? We use invisible paint in the factory?"

"Let me make this clear, if I can . . ."

"Oh, we use clear paint then," said Deeton. "Varnish, I suppose. Just as a protective coat."

"Protective coat," said the black teacher. "I see." And he and Deeton had a little smile together.

But then Deeton was up again. "What if the car won't run?"

"I beg your pardon?"

"What if, after we throw all this money and all these wonderful raw materials and assembly line workers into this thing—what if it won't run?" Definite gadfly.

"Oh, it will," said Dr. Shirley Knott, "because we are a goooood factory."

"What if the raw materials are defective to begin with? What chance has the assembly line then?"

"Does someone else have a question?"

Someone suggested robotics. Someone asked how the Special Ed. Industry fit in. Someone asked about fire drills. And someone asked about standing by your door. The meeting was memorable. Forgettably so.

But politicians and the public liked the factory thing. Why should we not expect a good "product" after "processing" if we gave money and built physical plants and hired assembly line workers?

He could have gone on like that. Often did. But this time a voice inside him said, "Lighten up, Sherm. That was all a long time ago. Besides, you never got paid as much as a factory worker, so forget it."

Dr. Shirley Knott felt so good about the factory in-service that she returned the next week with one on "Sensitivity About Anti-Personnel Weaponry"—at school. The kiwi group made a collage with little cardboard knives, guns, and grenades. Can you say, "Grenades"?

Chapter Six

Factories in general must be full of all kinds of people trying to do their best to crank out a good product. Mr. Sherman was certain also that his factory days were involved with a"product" that was a candidate for remediation. He had found himself trying to apply paint to teflon: to get some language skills into kids who were conditioned to resist any kind of mental stimulus.

"Some things, Mr. Sherman, are just not to be controlled." Ah, the scent of lime, tequila . . . Friday, Jerry, salt. "Did you ever notice who it is that most of us end up with in class?"

"You mean after they've skimmed off the talented, the brilliant, and the connected?"

"Yeah: after the 'Major Works'—code for 'smart'—sub-code for 'white'—and the kids who get into those classes because of the Inclusion rules, slow or not."

"Well, just kids, I suppose. One way or another, they take the smart ones away to special classes."

"We do not have ability grouping anymore, Mr. Sherman. It has been shunned."

"It has been re-named."

"Everything has been re-named. But my point is, in the mainstream classes . . ."

"Please don't say 'mainstream'—we've got food here."

"Sorry. In the regular classroom we have a nice mix: a kiddo or two from just about everywhere on the planet—except Eskimos, of course. And they're all good kids, I suppose . . ."

"Yeah, I suppose. Well, I've got one little rotter that I'd like to geld—but mostly, yeah, they're good kids, against all odds."

"Just average, run-of-the-mill kids."

"Yeah: normies."

"Now, Mr. Sherman, there is officially no such thing as Normal. Psychology 101. But passing—C's and B's—not too excited about this thing called Edjamakation. Just going along with the gag."

"Yeah. Normies! Gotcha. Go ahead."

"Well, now that we have sorted out the semantics . . ." offered Colleen.

"Never mind," said Jerry. "Ever notice that there are no government programs and consequently no government money for Normies?"

"There must be. Every dollar is earmarked for some specific scam!"

"Program! We call them Programs, Mr. Sherman. You are a man of words. You shock me! Scam, indeed!" And about here, Jerry would take a thoughtful sip and do his open-handed downstroke on his mustache and beard, then eyeball Mr. Sherman significantly.

"Okay. Program. Press on!

"Well, all of the programs are aimed either high or low—or somewhere off to the side of . . . uh . . . . 'Normal.' But if you want to know what is Normal, Normal is where the money doesn't go. You have Programs for the super-smart kids, Programs for the slower kids . . ."

"Dumb ones . . ."

"We don't call them dumb. Politically incorrect."

"Christ! Just get on with it!" said Colleen. Gees. Impatient!

"We take care of the drop-outs, too, the parolees, the drug addicts, the orphans, the misfits, the psychos, the sociopaths, the mentally and physically handicapped . . ."

"As it should be."

"As it should be, yes; but Programs! You have no mother? We have a program! You have no father? We have a program. Hungry?"

All together: "Program!"

"Pregnant?"

"Program!"

"Sixteen with three kids?"

"Program!"

"We have a nursery in the school! But my point is, if you are any kind of minority, domestic or foreign, poor or just twisted, there's program money."

"But there's no money for the Normie—no Program!"

"If someone does not fit anyone's profile of 'needing,' he is officially, financially, not there."

"Oh, it's not like they're not there," Colleen would say.

"But there is no Program. No money."

"I want money for my Normies," said Mr. Sherman.

"Not only that, but when was the last facruelty get-together where we split up into color-coded groups and listed all the ways to engage the minds of the normal kid? It's not done."

"And crystal apples! Nobody gets crystal apples for handling the Normies. Advanced and remedial—and bottom feeders."

"Bottom feeders. My God." Colleen was sensitive.

"I didn't mean to offend. I'm talking about the twisted, depraved, nasty, scummy little criminals—the felons . . ." said Mr. Sherman.

"That's better!"

"But no money and no Program for those in the middle,

and no acknowledgment. If you told 'Them'—the 'Big Them'—that you were shooting for the kid in the middle, they would come after you with a club."

"Well, guilty! That's where I aim," said Darby.

"Me, too—the Normie. I have to. I have 180 of them."

"Yes, yes—we all feel sorry for you."

"But if there is no Program, the kid does not exist! Hence, the whole midsection of the student body is not there. We have just put in another week of whatever we are doing, with no program money!" Jerry sipped.

"Okay, guys: you've lost the thread here. Tell you what, let's write up a proposal for a grant to address the special needs of the Normal!" Colleen's idea.

"I'm too busy. I've got 180 kids."

"I think it's against the rules," said Darby.

"But sometimes the needs of the many outweigh the needs of the few—or something like that," said Jerry, resident Trekky.

"I want money for the Normies!"

"To hell with all of them. We need more chips here."

"Damn. We strayed off the topic that day," Mr. Sherman mused. "And nothing was ever done! We were onto something."

How he missed the gang. And the salt. It was never the Margaritas. Probably.

That was what Friday was all about. Maybe it never solved anything—certainly not the problem of the disenfranchised Normie. Almost illegally, teachers aimed their efforts at that middle kid, at least Mr. Sherman did. But, hey, what does the average kid need, right? The computer came along, and you just ditched the kid in front of the screen and he was taken care of: no problem.

Right. Columbine and Jonesboro and Paducah seemed

far away from Mr. Sherman's warm little snowstorm—not in actual miles, but in days and months and years. He suspected that a lot of old teachers stared out their windows a long time thinking about those places. The kids who had acted out in those places were mostly those middle kids, undetected as problem kids. Old teachers would be brooding: Could I have helped, had I been there? Could I have prevented? Would one of these kids have liked me well enough to reconsider the human race and not try to kill everybody? How many times was I someone's island—without knowing it?

Colorado spun in. Snow. Up on that mountain out of Durango. Mr. Sherman went back there now—to a big A-Frame on that mountain, alone at Christmas with all those damn research papers. A little skiing, and then solitude and a pile of papers—alone between marriages, when the prospective ladies went home to their families and he lucked into a nice mountain lodge freely given by a friendly, sane buddy. It was going so well, too. 8:00 P.M., Mountain Time.

Mr. Sherman was plowing through the pile of papers, feeling a little sore on one hip from skidding down a few yards of ski slope, but otherwise okay. And then, stapled right in the middle of the paper, a note.

> Mr. Sherman:
> By the time you get to this, I will be dead.
>
> I hope you like the paper. I just can't go on with this stupid life.
>
> You were a good, fun teacher. It isn't that. Ciao! I'm out of here.
>
> Love,
> Chuck

P.S. Macbeth rules!

Panic. No phone number! Was there even a phone? If so, where? And did it work? Or was this a joke? Time to hit the panic button, but where *was* the panic button? He actually considered calling his ex-wife. He remembered that number. Found the phone. Got a dial tone. But now, who? He hung up. Information. Maybe the kid had chickened out. Maybe it was too late. The principal! Someone. It was probably over already. My God—two days after Christmas. Vacation half gone. Dead kid somewhere. Why me? For terrible seconds he was stunned and almost out of control—like his skiing—plummeting. Snow woman on the deck—right in the middle of the agony, he remembered seeing that silly snow woman. He was so safe out there—away from all the screaming school crap. And what else was in that stack of papers? What if he had looked through all of them at school before leaving and checked for suicide notes? Everything at once: the inane, the insane, and the automatic.

He found a faculty list in his briefcase, and , after a couple of glitches, he was talking to the principal. This was her job, too. She would make other calls and call him back—but she had not heard of any suicides. They hung up, and it was done. The panic button had been found. All he could do had been done. Passive verb! Damn. Doing what you can do and letting go is what teaching is all about. But, damn!

That was a moment! He remembered the minutes of waiting for the principal's call-back. Endless. He considered trying to grade papers. Instead, he riffled through the rest of them, looking for more notes—more trouble. He went over the kid's case in his mind. Nothing. Just a good kid—a nice kid, well-adjusted, it seemed. Not a clue—no signals to go on. A kid right out of the big middle of the gang of Normies. He did some hard staring out into the snow, and he resolved to knock the snow woman apart in the morning. The ridiculous has no business appearing alongside the painful. Or, not. What the hell.

In fifteen minutes the phone rang, and it was over. The kid had delayed, according to the principal, and he was still alive! Relief. Anger. Shame. The kid had survived Christmas and his parents had reconciled. Reconciled! Who knew? The kid knew. But nobody knew of his anguish—least of all, the school. But he *had* put it off, and now the immediate problem was over. There would be help—therapy, probably. All that in the minutes it took to tell it.

It was not as if any special training had taken over or anything! My God, he had stood there with the phone, hung it up, picked it up again, fumbled and floundered, stumbled and bumbled. But that was the fast part—seconds only! The endless fifteen minutes of waiting—that was the tough part. All the "Why me? What did I do right, and when?" Somehow, somewhere along the way, he had done something right and good—probably as a matter of routine each day, and he had made a difference to that kid. And between the impulse and the act, Mr. Sherman or the image of him had slowed things down just enough. He was a hero suddenly. He was loved. He was on the side of good.

Or, maybe the kid just chickened out.

But someone way back in college was right: you never know who you'll reach as a teacher, and you teach with every act.

Damn! What terrible things had he taught!?

Maybe that night had something to do with Mr. Sherman's curiousity about the next ten minutes—or his belief that he could fix things, save the day at the last minute. He loved to worry and complain, but he always believed he could win.

But there was no maybe about the papers. He would

never be enthusiastic about them. They were mine fields. They had burn-out written all over them.

That night on the Colorado mountain had gone on and on. There is adrenalin involved with finding a suicide note. And confusion. All those feelings at once—and almost calling his ex-wife: what was that all about? "You know what I'm sensing here?" he heard that counselor saying. "I sense conflict."

"Shut up."

No truly great teacher ever said "Shut up." That's a rule.

Mr. Sherman had almost done something else that night in Colorado. He had almost jumped in a car and headed straight for California. He felt for a moment that he no longer knew who he was. Maybe he had been alone too long; maybe he was influenced by the fact that his stack of research papers had gone supernatural on him and no longer cast a shadow or a reflection—only a peculiar aura. Whatever. He was coming down with a genuine identity crisis: Who am I? What am I? What am I for? Am I enough? In those days, when you didn't know who you were, you went to California. Today it would be Seattle. Maybe it was the snow woman, or the very fact that he had made one. Anyway, he almost went. But the snow stopped him: his pathetic car would not move. So he decided whoever he was would have to wait for himself in California. And he entertained the idea that he had fallen harder than he thought that day on the slopes. He went to bed. Tomorrow would be a day of green slopes. No more of this bunny nonsense.

Tomorrow. He moved over to the sliding glass door and touched base with the present. It was a real snowstorm now: real, wind-driven, opaque snow, nothing floating down now, all goal-oriented slashing white projectile snow—the kind that stings you when it hits you. And he was up in the night, and so pleased.

He let his eyes search out into the chaos; he stared, varied the focus again, tried the trick, expecting the image of something to pop out at him. But the whole thing reminded him of something else. In old black and white movies, directors loved to show the blur of rolls of newsprint speeding through the giant presses. And the headlines would come spinning at the audience: "George Raft Jumps Off the Brooklyn Bridge!" or "Bulldog Kline Gets the Chair."

But the headlines were different now. "Teacher Accused in Hugging Incident!" and "Teachers Indicted in Grocery Cart Theft!" and, spinning right at his face, "Marine Colonel Snaps Teacher's Neck for Ignoring Child!" And finally, "Peasants With Pitchforks March on Hugh Stone High! English Teacher Sought." Enough of that.

It could have been almost that bad: "English Teacher Snaps Kid's Neck in Hallway Fray!" But Mr. Sherman had always been able to prevent disaster with a last-minute adjustment—a correction. In Washington, they call it "spin." He had been able to defend every action with a good, hasty story. And he had been lucky a few times. So his guilt now had a lot to do with "almosts" rather than actual disasters. This guilt was not the arrogant thing he had earlier thought: not associated with quitting early and depriving Education of his services. It was about getting away with things.

"Well . . . ?"

Mr. Sherman turned away from the snowstorm, and there was the shrink again, sitting quite comfortably in the recliner, having a terrible time with his piccadilly. That was the confusing thing about him: part of him comfortable, part of him struggling. And he still looked like trusted and untrusted familiar men, mostly Bard this time.

"Well, what?"

"Woulds't thou purge thy soul of guilt? Thou hast a burden thou must lay down or break thy back."

"I don't want to hear any more about breaking backs. I was no worse than most. All right, I was not an intellectual. I took some short cuts. *Cliffs Notes.* I'm not all that smart, you know."

"I know."

"Shutteth uppeth! I'm not even sure I had a philosophy. I just found that everything they wanted me to do was not me—and it alienated my kids. So I shut the door and did it my way. Then I got up a phony scenario when they came to visit my class, and the kids cooperated. We had a lot of laughs about that. Then I tried to fit everything into some part of The System's latest substitute for thinking. And, if they caught me, they didn't let on."

"Thy oppressors, perchance, were thy allies?"

"Yeah. The enemy wasn't in the building: it was higher up. It wasn't even in the administration."

"Ah, thy Think Tank invention!"

"You bet. But was it an invention? We were trained to think in terms of "rationale"—rational bases for everything. Had to write it all down. Why would I not come up with the Think Tank as the logical explanation for all the illogical, paradoxical bull that came our way? It was too good, too consistent, too detailed to be accidental or serendipitous or random."

"Serendipitous. That was not yet a word . . ."

"It came along later. But there was a conspiracy. Do you know what a miracle a day at school is—if it works? Each kid has to be dragged out of bed, dressed, put on a bus, and physically deposited at the school. He wants to sue his parents for that—and the bus driver and the school. Then he has to be put into his classroom after being scanned and searched. He wants to sue the security people, the principals, and the teachers. Then he has to be contained: locked in, physically prevented from leaving, cut off from the dope dealers (or his customers, whatever), protected from gunmen roving the halls. He wants to sue the teachers for that—and the manufacturers of doors and locks. Then he has to be entertained—laugh a minute, riveting discourse, audio/visual aids, games, technical enhancements, state-of-the-art goodies all the way—anything the fire department, the EPA, the ACLU, and the PTA will allow: In antiseptic, non-sexist, politically correct, non-violent, non-religious, stone-ground, acid-washed, whole-grained, non-allergenic perfection—with wings!"

"Stop! *Thou* art driving *me* mad!"

"Sleep no more! Macbeth doth murder sleep . . . sleep, that knits up the raveled sleeve of care . . . death of each day's life . . . great Nature's second course . . . balm of hurt minds . . . "

"That was good, was't not?"

"'Twas! 'Twas indeed—verily and forsooth! Point is, I had to shut 'em out, shut the kids in with me, and make my case. The Bastards spent goodly buckage training us as 'Teams': and there were no teams. We went away—our separate ways. In the room there? It was I!."

"'Twas ever thus."

"Yes. But why, then, did they insist that there was help—jump up and down and scream that there was a team somewhere, some kind of help somewhere—tell the world that the 35 kids in our classes were not there . . ."

"Didst thou let them down?"

"The kids? Sure. Students don't fail—teachers fail! Where have you been, Bill? They carved that on the damned walls! No, goddammit. I did not fail. They were a great audience, and I played it to the hilt. I sang and danced and paced and pranced, I made them laugh and cry . . ."

"Didst thou get them all?"

"Well, no."

"Didst thou want them all?"

"Damned straight. I wanted to win them all. And when I didn't connect, when one of them didn't like me, I felt it and it hurt. There were just too damned many for too damned long."

"Ah'm gonna drop this psychiatry scam, Son. Y'all really burnt out. Color me gone." As the shrink turned into Ol' Billy Joe et cetera, he faded away to a vapor.

"That was a mean thing," said Mr. Sherman, "but it served its purpose."

The room was empty. The phantom shrink was gone, whatever he was, good or bad. "When you're driving your shrink crazy, and when your therapist has multiple identities, you might consider the possibility that you are not fully awake. Better check it out." And now he was talking to himself.

Better that than talking to an invention and getting replies, perhaps.

Yeah. A little nuts. He missed the kids, even the ones whose hobbies included self-mutilation, arson, cyber-sabotage, shoplifting, witchcraft, or mass murder.

And there was no relief at home. Toward the end there, Wifey had set up a fish tank to calm his nerves; however, he had become involved, worrying about the big ones eating the little ones, about the guppies vs. the angel fish, about someone spawning right there in front of him. It was all too stressful. The fish tank didn't work out.

Chapter Seven

Mr. Sherman was sure that he was fully awake. This was not going to be some cheap trick where he dreamed half of it and chalked the rest up to paranoia. If this was madness, he was ready to make the most of it. So why not trot The Bastards out and "get it on"?

It was surprisingly easy now. Dialogues with demons were alliterative *and* therapeutic, and now he successfully conjured up the whole Think Tank and arrayed them in the living room.

"But you ain't nothin' but a little bitty ol' pissant English teacher. What you doin', Boy? You ain't even supposed to know the Think Tank exists."

"I figured it out. You over-played your hand."

"Uh . . . he did pass all of the tests," Ol' Minnie Mae had to admit, "and he was around for a dozen 2-year, 5-year plans, and he administered a thousand tests that we sent down there."

"Hit almost all of the In-Services, too," Ol' Shirley Knott would have to say. "Always seemed enthusiastic, in his way. Preferred to be with the Puce group—or the cranberry. Sometimes quality butcher paper input. Can you say *input*?"

"Are you kidding? I was one of your white rats! You zapped,

I twitched. I ran your mazes. I walked your tightropes. Hell, I patty-caked, ran in tight circles, made up lies about myself, violated every code I believed in, gave up my manhood, my identity, my self-respect . . ."

"Oh, it's you! Ol' Mr. Sherman! Heard about y'all. Ain't nobody nowhere been through more o' our crap. We 'bout had yo' hide on that merit pay dido!"

"Will you please get off that while you are in my house?"

"Git off what, Son?"

"All that down-home, double-negative, fractured grammar routine. You are an educated man, and you should be able to handle a simple English sentence or two. And a few pure diphthongs, for Chrissakes, should be within your range. And you don't have to call everybody 'Son' and 'Boy'! Nobody is impressed with this Rebel Rube persona. And the Big Stetson and the string tie! You're not Garth Brooks and you're not Slim Pickins."

"But ah'm here to annoy y'all, Son! It's what ah do! 'Sides, nobody hahrd y'all tuh brang English tuh the South—y'all was jist put here to piss off others we wanted to annoy."

"And I lasted 27 years, too."

"Pissed 'em off fer 27 years. Hell, boy, you wuz workin' fer US!"

"I was an instrument you used to annoy my immediate superiors?"

"Go back and ask any of 'em. Hell, sometimes they didn't know what they wuz gonna do to save yo' bacon!"

"I was a burden then? All that time?"

"Hell yes. They had y'all for talkin' dirty in class, huggin' that pretty girl, printin' insensitive stuff in the yearbook, bitin' the hand that fed y'all . . ."

"I did *not* talk dirty in class!"

"Whole lecture on Hell's Canyon Dam day after the In-Service on Cussin' in School. Had yuh, Boy! Coulda kicked yo' tail good."

"And I *was* sensitive, damn you!"

"Great big black boy came to your class: big tall kid, plump, jolly, nice kid! And what did you say?"

"I know I spoke to him."

"You said, 'Who rubbed a lamp?' You call that sensitive?"

"Oh. That kid. Well, he looked like a genie to me."

"Coulda kicked yo' ass fer that!"

"But I won him! He became my instant friend!"

Without blinking, Ol' Billy Joe et cetera abruptly headed in another direction. Why not?

"Son, y'all jist take things too serious. We's just funnin'. Y'all cain't be thinkin' this wuz all some kind o' sincere effort."

Mr. Sherman had now stumbled upon the core thought. Maybe the core thought of his life. "Which part of the whole thing—my career—was the joke?"

Ol' Billy Joe et cetera spat out a stringy dark bolus into Wifey's fern. Then he laid it on him. "All of it, Boy."

"Don't make me get my wife up, damn you! You spit in her fern and she'll tear you a new one!"

"Hear me, Boy: your whole career was the joke! All of it. Ever day of it. Whole damn thing. How 'bout that!"

Quite a blow to hit you in the middle of the night after you've hung it up and crawled off into the hills! Mr. Sherman was stunned—numbed.

"So there never was any real effort to educate the kids? To teach? To make a difference in all those lives?"

"Well, ah cain't say whut y'all wuz doin'—but what we had in mind was kinda like babysittin'. Folks wanted them kids outa the house! What with all the crud we threw at y'all, nobody was expectin' anythin' more than containment."

"Containment."

"Sure! Warehousin', Boy! Jist hold onto the li'l bastards durin' the messy part o' the day—keep 'em the hell out of people's faces. . . . . If we'd a wanted 'em educated, we'd have done it different . . . . Git a grip, Boy!"

"Then I was right."

"Why else would we scrap a system that already worked! Shucks, boy, your great granny knew how to teach! We jist ditched all that to piss y'all off."

"Perhaps I can explain," offered Dr. Harm—not wishing to contradict, only to add to his mentor's thoughts. "Look, it has always been felt, on one level or another, that kids should be impounded until puberty is over, to make life in this world easier for all. That is what school is. Check the structure of the thing. You were just one of the guards. Rather average, actually."

Mr. Sherman was quiet, but thinking. Even his cynical invention of the Think Tank had not included this. Had this invention gone out of control? His lower lip began to tremble.

"Now, don't go tuh bawlin', Boy! Damn. Where's yer sense o' humor?" And then there was a change in Ol' Billy Joe et cetera. "Look, I'm going to abandon this facade for a while. I am weary." He tossed his Stetson aside and loosened his string tie. "It's just us here. The point is, the whole complex system of impossible barriers was put in place to make the lives of teachers miserable, while crippling our children's minds."

"It's that simple?"

"Honest to god. Our purpose from the beginning was to make your life sort of a mildish living Hell—so that one day you would withdraw from the scene, so to speak, and doubt forever that you ever did any good. Great plan."

"And it worked," said Mr. Sherman.

"I think so—rather well, actually. Look at you: you are here in the hills, away from the action—even got out with most of your honor—got lots of crystal apples . . ."

"Never mind the goddamned crystal apples!"

"Such language. I take it, then, you were in it for the money!"

"I thought it was a worthy thing . . ."

"Maybe you could not *do*, so you taught. How about that!"

"I have a damn good notion to snap your neck, you sonova—"

"Now, now, Mr. Sherman, no more fantasies. You never snapped anybody's neck—probably couldn't. And when that "mommy" came flying at your face across that table, you did nothing. She'd probably have whipped your butt anyway."

Billy Joe et cetera came closer now. The horns on the sides of his head became visible in the shadows. The smell of brimstone was strong. At least that was what brimstone should smell like.

"Boy, y'all jist easy," he said, grabbing his Stetson. "All y'all idealistic types is easy! Y'all got no sense o' humor, Boy?" All of them were fading through the wall now. But Ol' Billy Joe et cetera turned, smoldering a little. And, with a grin, he shot a thought into Mr. Sherman's heart.

"By the way, Boy, all those others? They wuz me, too." And he was gone.

But Mr. Sherman saw them all out under the yard light, dancing like imps, circling. They had jerked his chain again. And Mr. Sherman admitted it: he was easy.

He decided that this was going to be their last night. He would dispatch the Think Tank as part of the healing—right after he found out what was meant by that last remark: *They wuz me, too.*

"Someday, that Think Tank you've dreamed up will rise up and bite you, Mr. Sherman," said Jerry. "Be very careful" He remembered that Friday, the dark bar, the Margaritas, the salt.

"I will keep them under control, Sir. Without them I would go crazy prematurely. They explain things to me during this brief struggle when sanity seems important. Someday, I will be able to turn them loose. Or kill them off."

"And on that day you will surrender to madness?"

"Naw. I'll think of something to pull my jewels away from the flame. I created them; I'll get rid of them."

"When you no longer need them?"

"I guess so. Why all this concern about my Think Tank?"

"Well, lately you have made them sound so real! It's as if you've been communicating with them. That could be dangerous, my friend."

"I have to develop some of them further, of course; but they are very real. You would believe in them, too, if they sent you E-mail. E-mail is real to you; the Think Tank is real to me."

"Not the same thing. I did not dream up E-mail."

"Someone did."

"E-mail is interactive."

"So is the Think Tank."

"My God, Mr. Sherman, do you talk to them?"

"Right after Margarita #3! It's a great comfort. I blame them for the papers. I make it all impersonal: they're doing this to all of us. It's not just me."

That was toward the end of things in the city. Jerry's son was an ace computer jock and had him all hooked up with the entire world before the rest of the world joined up. Colleen was techy, too, and so was Darby. Mr. Sherman remained willfully computer illiterate. To him, Dot Com meant Communism.

"When you go off to the hills to rot, how will you keep in touch?" asked Colleen.

"Snail mail. I will write letters, lick stamps, all that. The stage comes through those parts twice a week."

"But who will drink your share of the Margaritas and hold your share of the truths to be self-evident?"

"I shall have to catch up—on those rare occasions when I come back into the city for ammo and beans and flour—and of course, salt!"

"We shall miss your smiling face," said Darby. "I believe you smiled once in 1987."

"Oh, that. Well, the queso was good that day, and, if I

remember right, the joke was mine." He was proud of his guarded reaction to humor, and resented it in others.

"All right, it's time for today's main order of business," said Jerry. "Do you realize that this is an anniversary for us?"

"Anniversary? I'll drink to that!"

But the girls were more curious. "Which anniversary? You are our historian, and I'll take your word for it, but . . ."

"And it is the beginning," Jerry said, "of the end." And he sort of rumbled the last words.

"Another round!" Mr. Sherman wanted to be prepared for this one.

"Colleagues, I suggest that we drink to the memory of our intellects, for, as of this very afternoon, we are no longer certifiably literate." And he drank. And they all drank.

"Oh, you don't mean The Test!?" Mr. Sherman was fast.

"Five years ago we passed a test that indicated that we would be literate, if we passed, for a period of . . ."

"Five years! By God, he's right!"

"There has been no follow-up test. So we could all go home today and get a nasty letter declaring our literacy null and void."

"I say we drink to the void! Or the null. Whatever." Mr. Sherman's salt craving was strong.

"A toast, then, to our literacy. It was good while it lasted!" And they sipped.

"Wait a minute," said Darby as a wave of inspiration struck her. "Monday morning I'm going into the office and turn myself in. I can no longer function if I can't read and write. Besides, there's a rule about literacy, and rules have to be observed."

And she did. She also reminded the office that there was supposed to have been a math test, too, but it had never happened. This was hardly fair to math teachers. Apparently, however, the Ph.D. had already gone to the literacy test person, and the strings had been tightened—probably to annoy some specific person. But Darby had her day. There was a bulletin about it.

Bulletin: All teachers who passed the literacy test five years ago are hereby re-certified.

So shut up already.

The lyrics of a modern song now began to cycle through Mr. Sherman's semi-conscious brain: "Whoa whoa, yeah yeah . . ." followed by something he could not comprehend at all. This happened often. "I wanna tell yuh, Baby: Whoa whoa, yeah yeah yeah." What could it mean?

It was probably his own fault. He had allowed himself to struggle for years with, "The loose is up where we belong . . ." or "The loop was up where we belong . . ." Certainly no officer or gentleman would inflict such punishment, but there it was in the movie. That puzzle had been solved by students who found words on an album cover.

He missed the kids sometimes. They could tell him what "Whoa whoa" meant, and probably who "Baby" was; and he could get back to Keats and Wordsworth and Shakespeare.

Chapter Eight

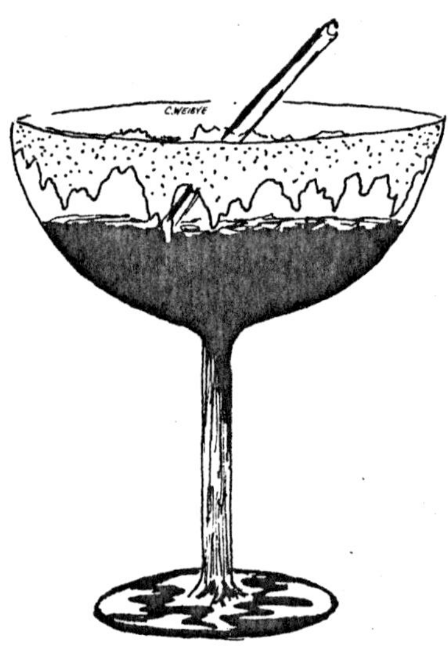

The shrink was back, looking less and less like the bust in the Stratford church and more and more like someone real. He had a blemish or two. The left side of him was not quite like the right side. He had not been re-touched. And he was holding a laptop computer, and he seemed to have bifocals, like Jerry. Like Mr. Sherman himself—and nearly everyone in the mountains.

"Let *me* quote *thee*, Mr. Sherman. These words are thine: 'I am sorry, class, but MY dog ate YOUR homework.' Didst thou speak thus?"

He knew about it immediately. Mr. Sherman had a good memory. Too good, perhaps. "I could not tell them the truth."

"Explain thy position and relieve thy burden!" It was a command.

"I had destroyed their papers because of the horrible scene I had interrupted in my living room. I had to destroy those papers, but I could not tell the students why. So, I borrowed their trick and blamed the dog."

"What horror didst thou see—some apparition? Some ghost? What hideous spirit?"

"Nay! No. They were breeding—right there in the living room by my recliner—a reeking, perverse pile of them, squirming out of their rubber bands and writhing there together on the carpet, exchanging inks and pencil leads, twisting lustily in ecstatic abandon . . ."

"Thy students?"

"No—the papers. The ungraded papers: breeding, multiplying, compounding! It had to be stopped."

"Ah, brave new world . . ."

"Damn straight! I gathered up the whole disgusting lot of them and threw them into the fireplace and burned them up."

"Uh . . . preposition . . ."

"But you can't go to class and tell the kids that their papers were making the beast of two backs there on the floor!"

"Didst thou see what thou sayest thou saw, or was't a false creation of the heat-oppressed brain?"

"The papers were humping! More and more of 'em every

minute—piles and piles of them! I had to act, or they would have taken over my house, my life, my soul. And the fire marshal had already said they were a fire hazard."

The shrink plicked away on his laptop, putting together another play or sonnet, no doubt.

"Thou hast saved thine own soul then, by lying?"

"More than once!"

"Didst thou not fling large piles of such papers down a flight of stairs, and thus grade them on elevation?"

"That was a joke! None of us ever really did that, but when papers threatened to drown us, we thought of the stairs—A's for the top step papers, F's for the bottom .... But I would never have done it that way. I would have gone to the bottom and flung them up! The weighty ones would have gone to the higher steps. It would have been more fair."

More plicking.

"Take care in thy jests, lest thou be taken for a jester. Late or soon, thou wilt reap what thou seweth. God, I'm good at this stuff."

"Well, if this is going to be a confession session, let's get on with it. I'm going to be cured by morning, anyway. Want to know my big secrets?"

"Thy deepest and thy darkest."

"All right. How's this: I made my lesson plans after the lessons were over."

"I know the strategem."

"They wanted the plans in advance—plans that would be obsolete the minute they were written down. You could draw up two weeks of plans if you wanted, but they would drop in with tests or workshops or fire drills—run in something about sex or AIDS or drugs—and the whole plan would be blown. So, I dropped back. At the end of the semester I had lovely plans, all drawn up after the fact. 'Do it today, plan it tomorrow!' That was my secret."

"I wrote plays while they were being rehearsed."

"Not *Macbeth.* It's too tight."

"Thank you."

"But enough of you: back to me! Did you know that I actually had to go to a window shade seminar?"

"Thou liest!"

"Nay. 'Tis sooth I say! They came into my room and found my window shades uneven and slapped my ass into a seminar on keeping window shades level—across the whole side of the room—with 35 screaming kids yanking at them!"

"Ah, thy rage!"

"And you may not know it, but the very best people in the business put together some of the best lesson plans ever written and they were published with corresponding textbooks for all teachers to use—and then we were forbidden to use them, and forced to write up our own!"

"Window shade lesson plans?"

"No, you're getting it mixed up."

"And losing interest."

"But you're my shrink!"

"And losing consciousness . . ." And Big Bill's image fell asleep, right there in Mr. Sherman's chair.

Outsiders just can't appreciate the agonies of people in jobs they've never held. A plumber would probably fall asleep listening to an accountant; a teacher would probably fall asleep listening to a flight attendant. Mr. Sherman could hardly blame his shrink.

The Regulator clock with the screwed-up hands struck 2:38 A.M. and roused Mr. Sherman, who had put himself to sleep, too. Behind his eyes, his brain or something was drawing into a tight knot—like drying chewing gum parked under a desk. Sinus tablets from WalMart would take care of that.

Mr. Sherman was reminded of another of his old

suspicions about schools. The student desks had to have been pregummed in the factory! He had seen new student desks arriving—whole new buildings and wings of buildings, spanking new with new desks. And always there was gum on the desks. It was the same way with broken glass and graffiti: in the newest restrooms there was immediate damage and destruction, wasted towels and toilet paper, graffiti. It had to come from the factory that way. It could not have been the kids: they did not do anything that well, that thoroughly, or that quickly: and never never that consistently.

"Consistency, consistency, consistency! Can you say 'Consistency'?" Of course there was a seminar on Consistency.

"Conformity!" shouted the Puce group.

What a day that had been! Absolute civil disobedience! The large group had divided again, and Mr. Sherman had been tossed in with acquaintances with Puce badges. And that was the day, way back at the beginning, when the Friday Margarita gang first met. Oh, they had known each other, but that day they had de-coded that word together and shouted it back in one voice. A little thread of rebellion running through the whole puce tapestry! It called for a toast, and there was nothing to drink at the facruelty meeting. And that was when they found the terrible little bar with the adequate chips, the sometimes salsa, and the great queso mostly. And they found each other.

"A foolish consistency is the hobgoblin of little minds," if Emerson said so, and he did. But it was the theme of that first meeting.

"They—the BIG THEY—Them—they want us to be consistent: to get the same thing from Mrs. McTrain as they get from Mr. Sherman—in the same way, every time," Jerry had declared, "that's all."

"And every kid should get the same treatment as every

other kid from no matter who he ends up with as a teacher. Every day, every room, all the way: must be taught the same, punished the same, rewarded the same, yada yada yada."

"I can't do that. I'm different," said Darby.

"I can. I have no personality of my own, no convictions, no ideas, no individuality. I can do it," said Mr. Sherman.

"Hmmmm. That is inconsistent with your reputation, Mr. Sherman," mused Jerry.

"Whom have you been heeding?"

"Hundreds. I've been heeding hundreds."

"I stand by my story—stubbornly, no matter how many hundreds you've heeded."

"Is this *Beowulf,* or what? My God!" Colleen never could relish minced words.

But then her eyes got big, the way they would from then on when she had something to toss into the "debate." "Listen: I walked by Mr. Deeton's room today. I looked in, and it was like looking at a still photograph."

"Black and white?" offered Jerry.

"No. It was just that nobody moved. Nobody blinked. Nobody spoke. Nobody turned a page . . . shifted his eyes . . . nobody breathed."

"Nobody dared," said Jerry. "That's Deeton's class."

"If that ever happened in my room, I would dance naked on the desk or something. It was frightening!" Colleen cringed.

"God, my room is like a beehive," said Mr. Sherman.

"Mine is like an execution—a hanging or the old guillotine routine," said Jerry.

"Let's get back to Mrs. O'Hara dancing naked on the desk."

"Never mind, Mr. Sherman! It won't happen. I could no more be like Deeton than you could be like me."

"I could be like you. I love those kids. I am sensitive, dammit, and don't you forget it! I'm so sensitive I make myself sick!"

"That's just the salsa. We need better salsa here, if we are to stay." And Colleen got better salsa, too. The salsa was fresh after that, as Mr. Sherman recalled, and the queso was great. Great.

"Suppose," offered Jerry, stroking his beard in the way that would become so familiar, "suppose that, like water, we as teachers could seek a level—arrive at a natural or agreed level. Consistency. Would that get us crystal apples?"

"I'm new to this level of thinking. What the hell is a crystal apple?"

"Huh. Virgin," grunted Darby.

That was the day Mr. Sherman found out about rewards in The System. Somewhere in the spare room under the little bed, there was a box, and his collection of crystal apples was there. Like his old track medals and his old service pins and Greek group pins—his World's Greatest Teacher plaque and his World's Greatest Lover Medal—all of it was in there somewhere. And nobody cared. Crystal Apples were something to hand you to balance out a ceremony on a boring afternoon in an after-school meeting. And yes, teachers would fight for them. Nowhere under Mr. Sherman's bed in that spare room was there a box of "sharp sticks in the eye."

Way back there at that first Margarita meeting, the gang saw that coming. It was a great meeting.

Another pensive session at the glass door. Another glance at Miss Whitby and her frosty cart. Still there, a sentinel in the night.

The night patrol at the Salvation Army Thrift Shop had just changed. Mr. Sherman and Miss Whitby had staked the joint out for two nights, starting right after the kids stole the wheels off her Safeway cart. The carts at the thrift shop were not the best, but the lighting was poor and the guard was 78 years old. The two of them had written up plans with ELO's galore. Mr. Sherman had blackened parts of his face.

He crept toward the dumpster downwind from the alert guard and checked his watch. "Hmmmm. 8:09 P.M. Almost time." He crouched and graded a few papers. 8:29 P.M.—the guard approached. Mr. Sherman leaped catlike from the shadows of the dumpster, grabbed the guard from behind, and snapped his neck. He tossed the grunting bundle into the dumpster and slid over the embankment into the bayou.

Miss Whitby brought the pick-up truck, and the cart was hers. Quick. Clean. Perfect.

"Grunting bundles. That's Stephen Crane," said Mr. Sherman as they drove away into the night. *"Red Badge . . ."*

"Right, Chief," she had said, the light of worship in her eyes.

He could have it that way if he wanted to. Little happenings like that could be inserted—like making up the lesson plans after class. His classes had looked like magic on paper: well-timed, balanced, perfect. Fact was, he had fished that grocery cart out of a bayou and sprayed the mud off it with a garden hose. But there's no romance in that—no drama. Nothing noble about it either. Better to think of it as stolen—or taken! Seized! Captured.

He looked out the sliding glass door again, and, of course, she was out there—just standing there in the snow with her Salvation Army Thrift Shop cart. Staring at him.

But then, he could see her there any night, with his eyes shut. Yes, yes, lighten up. That, too. But Mr. Sherman was a teacher and a fixer; and since he had not been able to fix Miss Whitby, he would now worry about it one more night. A luxury.

He resolved that, if he were ever to pull her away from the cubicle and get her to focus, he would tell her the other things he had learned. "Some people the kids will not allow to teach. There is a secret mark on those people that only kids can see, and those are the ones that are sent away crying—male or female, big or small, equal opportunity all around."

He had seen that a few times. It's like a pack of wild dogs tearing up some frightened doe.

And then there were the Mr. Deetons of the world. He could walk into a room full of the ghetto's worst savages—even Freshmen! and the clock on the wall would stop, and the blood in every vein in the room would stop cold, thrown erasers would freeze in midair, acne would dry up, spoons would bend, and there would be peace! Some said it was because he had once killed a kid and hung his carcass on a map hook above his blackboard; some said it was because when The Bastards came to him about dumbing it down he told them to go to Hell. Nobody knew what it was, but Deeton had it. He had enough of it for six or eight rooms at once. He frowned once and they had to paint his room the next day. But even he could not have helped Miss Whitby.

Subs, of course, were chopped up into little pieces by all of the kids—even the model students. It was a matter of tradition. Many lives were changed that way. Hugh Stone High had a reputation among subs, and it became difficult to obtain one even in an emergency.

In-Services on Empowerment, Discipline, Assertiveness, and Criminal Psychology died on the butcher paper hung on the wall. Fact is, teachers who really teach are *allowed* to teach, and those people have magic.

Miss Whitby had been given her shot. And she had been eaten alive and doomed to walk Mr. Sherman's midnights with that goddamn grocery cart. She was not anybody's fault.

None of this helped Mr. Sherman. It was a set of facts that he was able to understand intellectually but unable to use in the middle of the night to save his remaining mind. Still, if he could see her somewhere—not the phantom out there in the snow, but the real Miss Whitby, the E-Worker now—maybe he could tell her that it was okay for her not to be a teacher, that none of it was her fault, that the Think Tank had planned it, and the Think Tank was real, and the kids are cruel. And probably drive *her* nuts, too.

He could not resist. We took one more look. And she was still out there, the snow piling up around her and on her—a frozen corpse hanging onto a grocery cart, eyeballing him.

"Not your standard, garden variety curse," he thought. "A curse of literary proportions! This is getting good."

And he thought of the albatross.

He thought he had better occupy the recliner before another attack by the shrink, and so he plodded over to the thing and dropped heavily into it. It was not a good move, for it made the floor squeak and it made the chair squeak, and that could awaken his wife, and that would not be good. She had not seen him crazy since that one time in English traffic—and then only out of the corner of her eye, for she was driving. No, she must sleep, and he must stay awake and become sane by dawn. That was the plan. He held still.

But from the recliner, the wakeful view included the blank TV screen, always a curiosity. And playing now was the retirement party for Ol' Billy Joe et cetera himself.

He was weeping, and his Stetson was off, and his bald head was glaring, and he looked as he had always looked. This ceremony had taken place years ago. Other superintendents had come and gone since this moving scene, and he had operated from the dank sub-cellar, the reeking lair of the Think Tank.

"Ah cain't begin tuh tell y'all how proud ah been tuh serve y'all these many years. But ah got tuh go. A rockin' chair awaits me, and a trout stream. Ah leave y'all in good hands: a fahn lady, ah'm shore, comin' here from L.A. tuh hep y'all." At this point, he got so country Mr. Sherman could no longer follow the words. But the crying, the red neckerchief, the tears, the histrionics in general were memorable. Ol' Billy Joe et cetera's contract had been bought up by the 'Board for $475,000; he had been given a little farewell bonus of $250,000; and he had been hired as a consultant for the next five years at $125,000 per year. The tears were baffling.

But something popped into Mr. Sherman's mind at this point that had a strange aura about it. It reminded him of when he knew the answer to a *Jeopardy* question but could not quite cough it up. He looked hard at the blank TV screen, and time ran out. Ol' Billy Joe et cetera was addressing him. "Now, ahmo say this one more tahm, Son. Shouldn't hafta beat y'all over the head with it. Remember this?" He rolled his eyes and looked very significantly at Mr. Sherman. "By the way, Boy, all those others? They wuz me too."

Mr. Sherman had seen that before and he had heard that before. And even under duress, he had a good memory. Ol' Billy Joe et cetera had said those words to him earlier this evening right in this very room—and then just walked off through the wall. But "others"? What others?

"Damn, Boy, y'all disappoint me."

"Wait a minute! The other superintendents!!" Ol' Billy Joe et cetera was absolutely gleeful now. On the blank TV screen they started parading through: the lady superintendent from L.A., Dr. Bertha Nations, a "gee whiz" advocate (that is, she embraced anything new and different as good and vital, no matter what); then Dr. Elk Feather Running, Native American male from Michigan, a back-to-basics type who wanted fundamentals stressed all the way to graduation (sang bass, the only non-tenor tom-tom singer/dancer in North America); then Dr. Jason Hemings Jefferson, an Afro-American from Virginia who claimed rich roots in American history and soil (gee-whiz advocate again, pendulum swing thing).

Ol' Billy Joe et cetera applauded them one by one as news footage of each superintendent flickered away on the still dark TV screen. There was no sound except the applause—loud clapping, whistling, grunting, cheering—loud enough to wake the dead, or Mrs. Sherman.

"Shhhh! Quiet class! I mean, keep it down! You'll wake my wife."

"I'm not even here, Boy. Damn, Boy, get a grip!" With pride, he turned to his creations. "Ever one of 'em wuz me! Ol' Bertha Nations there wuz mah first drag performance! Ever wonder why they paid out hundreds of thousands of dollars in 'search' money to find a new supe? Ol' Harm's idea! He did the search! Then, after it was all spent and pissed everbody off, I jist put on that dress and took over."

"When you retired, you never left, is that correct?"

"Jist dropped the Ol' Billy Joe act and came up with Ol' Dr. Bertha. Hell, Boy, Chief of Security made a pass at me, I wuz so good."

"All those tears . . ."

"Hey, the tears wuz real! That retirement ceremony is always sad. I bawled like a baby. Bet you did, too."

"And that was an era of New Math and Whole Language . . . ?"

"Oh, Dr. Bertha—yeah. Then ah come up with Ol' Doc Elk Feather Running, and a swing the other way, toward the back-to-basics thing. Ever hear of an elk feather? God, I loved that. But y'all gotta give 'em variety. And make the teachers do the follow-through."

"Well, we had to do something. They couldn't read! It was time to go back to basics—but all the way through high school?"

"The Injun only lasted two years! Then it was time for a black leader. Boy, that wuz a make-up! I thought I'd tie him into that Jefferson mess with the slave girl. Either piss yuh off or make y'all feel warm an' fuzzy! Oh, how I luv it when a scheme comes together!"

On the TV screen the faces of the three superintendents

faded together into Billy Joe et cetera's face, and Mr. Sherman could see that it was all true.

"See, Boy—they all the same! All this outside stuff's just a window dressin'. At the bone, they all alike, just throwin' out there whatever gonna cause the most trouble at the tahm! Lotta change fer the sake o' change! Hell, ah'm proud to say y'all ain't seen the end of anythin' begun in the last 30 years—not on my watch!"

"But why did you go to the trouble of changing faces, names, image? Why bother?"

"Let me teach, Son. Let me teach you what you already know: What is the rule when the question is *why*?"

After a moment, Mr. Sherman dug it out. "Usually, they say to follow the money."

"There you go, Son. You ain't so dumb. Boy, ah got the salaries; ah got the search money; ah got the bonus money; ah got the consultant fees; ah sold surplus food, surplus machines; ah had jams and jellies goin' boy! The money. And, since nothin' worked, change was an easy sell—so we changed and changed, Son, and the more things change . . ."

"The more they remain the same."

"You wanna come out of retirement, Son? I might be able to use y'all."

"No, thank you. So it was all a circle—a treadmill—an exercise in futility . . ."

"And sooo expensive."

"But why couldn't we see it? I thought you went underground, but you just mutated!"

"Son, if y'all would like to know more about this program, just log onto the web and check us out at www.BJetc.com. And as he recited the long, slow "Dubya dubya dubya dot . . ." he began to fade, transforming into this superintendent and that, with electronic bleeps and tweedles, descending to one tiny white dot, and then gone.

The smell of brimstone again.

"I do not believe in devils," Mr. Sherman thought, "but I suppose that was what they were counting on all along." Believing depends upon experience. There would naturally be devils with madness—many devils! Devils outnumbering angels 35 to 1. The accustomed odds. You just have to reach a manageable little arrangement. It's all about perspective.

Or not. What the hell!

But something else was going on now. As he monitored the storm once more, Mr. Sherman felt a confusing and disappointing urge—subtle for a minute or two, then stamping its feet, waving its arms, yelling at him, demanding attention. Some primal voice in him was telling him to go outside, work his way down the stone steps he and Wifey had built out back, descend hundreds of feet into the woods below the first ledge, go down to the base of the cliffs and down further along the old logging road a mile or so in the dark, and then climb back up, with wind pounding snow into his face, and come back into the house a steaming apparition with foggy glasses, absolutely chilled to the bone, exhausted, nose dripping, frozen. Why? Heredity, probably, genetics, DNA!—some Minnesota thing. He remembered it now. Forty-five years out of God's Country, and the urge was still there. And this was something that he would definitely have to beat. He thought of the current cliché: "Don't go there!" He retreated from the window and the urge.

Another urge had to be dealt with—and soon. It had to be brief, and it had to be quiet. All that Diet Coke! He would avoid squeaky spots in the floor, tip-toe in, shut the door slowly, and do it sitting. No lights. No splash. No flush. Stealth tinkling!

It would be a critical mistake to awaken Wifey in the middle of the night and drag her into all of this. She might make him go to a doctor—or a real shrink. She was a problem solver, too, but she was ruthless. Chances were she would be narrow-minded about these urges.

He crept into the bathroom, made the hit, and got out clean: silent, swift, accurate. Then he returned to his vigil.

Plenty of snow on the deck now, but he could see where the spaces between the boards were. Perfect.

And off he spun again to Colorado, the A-frame uphill out of Durango, and the snow on the deck. Right there on the deck he had built that awesome snowwoman. Oh, he was no sculptor, but he packed and scraped and cut, trying to find the lovely body in the pile of snow, and, by the time he was able to quit working on her, she was a shapely entity: tall and delicate. He had done her from memory. Back then he remembered good things whenever possible. Yes, an alabaster goddess. A whim. No desperate thing, either—just a little joke. He would take pictures of her, maybe one of himself working on her, and say to his sick friends, "I was sooo lonely that . . ."

But he had forfeited any right to feel sorry for himself: this was self-imposed exile. He was alone at Christmas, between marriages, off on a cold Rocky mountain, trying to ski, all by choice. The A-frame would sleep twenty, but it is hard to get people to give up family activities at Christmas, even if it's a free gig. He was between families, in the void beyond divorce.

And it was going so well, too. But then, right in the middle of the pile of research papers, the kid's suicide note, the panic, the impulse to call, who else?—his ex-wife. "Aaaarrrgggh!"

"You know what I'm hearing here? I'm hearing conflict."

"Oh, shut up."

The Shrink now looked like a mirror image of Mr.

Sherman: absolutely ridiculous. And there it was again, the ridiculous right in the middle of the serious part.

"But that impulse, Mister. What was that? Have you thought about that?"

"Not a hell of a lot."

"Well, I don't see how we can go on with the cure here if we don't deal with that." The Shrink's voice was that of Mr. Sherman, too: tinny and thin, definitely not James Earl Jones.

"I almost called my ex-wife because I didn't have a new one yet. And I was alone, and nobody knows I did that. Almost did that."

"Well, which was it? Did you actually call her, or what?"

"No, I did not. I knew the number, you see. And, for several years, I had reached for her when I had problems. But I put the phone down. Ended up calling the principal, which was the right thing to do anyway."

"So . . . uh . . . who was this snowbabe?"

Nasty question.

"She was nobody. Just a sort of busty female shape. I couldn't do a face, really."

"Not your wife, then?"

"Not my wife. Ex-wife. Nor was it my new wife, whom I had not yet met. She was just sort of a Gang Busters babe! I was creating, you see; and I kept adding snow. It was supposed to be funny."

The shrink did not look amused. Mr. Sherman was looking at his own perpetual frown now—a crease ironed into his forehead by years of trying to look stern and trying not to laugh at any jokes but his own. Even the big glasses were there.

"When that terrible fifteen minutes of waiting was over, and you received a phone call from the principal telling you that the kid was still alive, what did you do to that snowwoman?"

"Well, I eventually kicked her to pieces—shoved the snow

off the deck."

"I'm not buying that. You hate to scrape frost off your windshield because you abhor the destruction of art. Tell me you tore down that snowwoman!"

Mr. Sherman was now in the presence of a demon who had been reading his mail: who had access to uncomfortable places in his mind and had less sympathy than God.

"Okay. I couldn't do it. There."

"So. But right after you talked to the principal and put the phone down: relieved, drained but still excited, confused, ecstatic and sad all at once . . . what did you do then?"

"I had some Jack Daniels Black Label . . ."

"Not that! Dammit, it's me here! You don't drink at all anymore, and you never were a real drinker. It would have been dramatic as hell, but you're not Bogart, you're not Lemmon . . ."

"I gave her a hug."

"What? Louder now."

"I gave the snowbabe a hug."

"You call that a hug?"

"I had great need of some sort of human contact. I was a mess there for a while. I was used to the bell ringing and two thousand kids running across my feet. I looked around, but of course there was nobody—nothing around with a human form. See what I mean?"

"Sure."

"I was shattered. Shredded. And alone with it."

"And so you hugged a snowwoman?"

"Okay: I went out there on that deck and I *held* her. I wrapped my arms around her, and I held on until I was cold. There."

"And you cried."

"Did not."

"Did too."

"Mr. Sherman Wept. You know, the shortest verse in the

Bible . . .”

“Shut up.”

“And you had thought yourself above all that.”

Maybe there was something wrong with the core thinking. Mr. Sherman had learned, sitting on the john one day reading GABB, that if a person brings a dream to life, he makes it mortal: capable of death. He hoped that it would work with nightmares. He speculated that by letting light and air and cold get to his tormentors, he might kill them. But this. Truth, right in there with the rest of it. This was too much. Only honesty could save him.

“Okay,” he said finally, “I’m just going to go ahead and admit here that . . . uh . . . that, now and then, I need someone.”

An explosive, unbelieving snicker from the Shrink. “You think?”

“Even if I have to make her out of snow.”

“The very thing.”

“We work with what we have.”

“In one way or another, that’s what we all do,” said the Shrink. And then he was gone.

Mr. Sherman felt warm now, and strong, and comfortable. All things had conspired to make him realize his humanity. Now what? It was snowing for all of the teachers and students in all of the world, as far as he was concerned, and he would enjoy morning for all who would miss the lovely day off. He resolved that he would turn on the TV very early and watch the crawl of the names of the lucky towns who would have a snow vacation, and smile. And maybe make a nice breakfast for Wifey.

He was fine now. Really.

Chapter Nine

Mr. Sherman's heart ached, and a drowsy numbness pained his sense, as if of hemlock he had drunk. It gets that way with Old English teachers in the middle of the night. "Oh, for a draught of vintage—a beaker full of the warm South . . ." Sleep. Sleep was crushing him, enveloping him, smothering him. But he must not sleep. His targeted "outcome" was: getting his act together by sunrise.

In the overpowering creeping anesthesia of it all, there came a familiar instant—an intimation—that made Mr. Sherman sit straight up and say out loud, "What was that?" He dampened his finger with Diet Coke and held it up, searching for a mild zephyr—a current of telling air. He flicked his tongue. He probed with all of his senses. It was there, all right; he knew this sensation well. A faculty meeting was coming down! One of THOSE meetings, timed to take advantage of the dismissal energy slump in mid-afternoon, when the teachers are drained of all energy and try to just hold still for a moment, trembling.

Soon, there was a principal. Mr. Sherman had never worked for a principal he hadn't liked. Principals seemed most blameless, really. Others felt other ways. In the stormy atmosphere of the school district, not everything that came down from above was rain. The usual stuff that flows downhill flows downhill in a school district. The principal was often the umbrella that kept the worst of it from hitting the teachers directly. There was always splash. But the principals were not the bad guys. Still, they had to have meetings.

This principal was female, and she said, "I have good news and bad—same old same old. So let's set up a buddy system right away. Please count off: 1, 2, 1, 2,—around the room from the left."

The entire faculty counted off. No mistakes, except for one coach, a rare visitor at faculty meetings, who wanted to be Number 3.

"Now, the one's keep the two's awake, and vise versa. This could be a little turgid. And please: do not grade papers."

There would be a rustle of papers at this point, a few grumbling mutterings, some readjusting and settling in.

"Okay, Item One: the test scores for the TMPP have arrived, and I regret to inform you that 47% of our student body is in the failure column. We have lost 2%."

A hand went up. "Mr. Deeton?" said the principal wearily, nodding at Mr. Deeton, who had risen at the back of the room.

"Madame," Mr. Deeton scolded, "the TMPP is a personality test: the Totally Mindless Personality Profile! How does one fail a personality test?"

"I am just sharing the results with you, Mr. Deeton. I do not care to get into the politics of the operation. They send us tests, we administer them, we send in the answer sheets, they report back."

"Thank you, Madame," said Deeton. He then sat down without the trace of a smile.

"I thank you, Mr. Deeton. And now, Item Two: Mrs. Grimshaw, on her rounds through the new wing, found a couple making love in the second floor girl's restroom. It was the second incident this month."

Almost everyone would know about such a thing, so there would hardly be a hubbub. However, a hand went up.

"Mrs. McTrain?"

Darby had that look again. "I believe that if everyone were to stand by his door this whole problem would go away."

Now there would be a loud moan.

"It is, after all, a rule. It is also a rule, although not a specifically written rule, that making love in the restroom is a no-no. I do think you have the boy on being in the girl's restroom, but that is as specific as the rules get. But, since it is not good to have the kids interacting in this way, standing by our doors—the answer to ALL problems of conduct—should do the job."

It made sense to Mr. Sherman, and he wanted to start up a chorus of "Stand by Your Door" right there, but there were no Margaritas, and people were tired.

"Thank you, Mrs. McTrain. But our real problem is that the Fire Marshal has informed us that the behavior is also a violation of the fire code."

Now there would be real input. God, how they loved input at faculty meetings! Advocation of abstinence would be one way; rest room monitors would be brought up again; sprinkler systems would be shunned as too tempting to the prankster; someone would mention "right to privacy," and possibly small cots—fireproof cots, of course.

"Item Three: Volunteers. When we have our next bomb threat, it will be necessary, after evacuation, for the building to be searched for bombs. All male faculty with military experience, please consider volunteering for that team. Also, any woman interested or especially qualified. Then, we need more participation in the Faculty Advisory Committee. As you know, the group does the vital job of relaying faculty 'concerns' to the administration. We then ignore them or act upon them, depending . . . I'll catch you later, Mr. Deeton . . . depending upon the political climate, and the time of the month." There would be a good chuckle here. The principals were good guys. "And one more volunteer thing: we need people to hand out condoms in class—preferably not the same people who are teaching abstinence, but not necessarily those teaching parenting skills. And no, not the coaches this time. The coaches have enough to worry about."

Mr. Deeton was called on again. "The Faculty Advisory Committee is a toothless, de-clawed kitten. I recommend that it be abolished." He sat down.

"Thank you, Mr. Deeton. We will approach that at our next FAC meeting." Small chuckle, maybe. "Miss Thurgood?"

"My shack leaks."

"That's 'temporary building,' Miss Thurgood."

"My 'temporary building'—that—that ramshackle collection of rotting timbers that has been there for 25 years—leaks. I had a box of ungraded papers destroyed the last time it rained."

Thirty hands went up.

"That is a maintenance problem, Miss Thurgood. Simply file Form #X711513L. Now, the rest of you: I know what this is about, but I will give the line to . . . Mr. Sherman."

"Thank you. I would like to store my ungraded papers in Miss Thurgood's shack, if possible."

"That's 'temporary building,' Mr. Sherman. And, sorry: No can do."

The other hands went down.

Mr. Sherman remembered those wonderful meetings, the struggle to stay awake, the harried principals, the little dramas, the cheap gags, and the sexual tension. Oh, yes, sexual tension: Would the Valedictorian this year be pregnant—or already a parent? Would the captain of the football team be hit with a paternity suit? Would some Palestinian boy get some Israeli girl preggers and cause a whole Romeo and Juliet soap opera at school; or would it happen with Irish Protestants and Catholics, Serbs and Bosnians, Pakistanis and Indians? All of the ripe little rascals were in school together at Hugh Stone High, bouncing off one another, and occasionally on one another.

A hand reached out and slapped Mr. Sherman awake. It was his own hand. He had always disciplined himself when he began having thoughts that were beneath him. Sometimes he slapped himself raw. He took inventory now: here he was, sorely missing faculty meetings after dreading them so—looking back with a degree of nostalgia. This had to be madness.

And then the "just once" syndrome hit him again. He could now go back and repair the damage of all those faculty meetings: clean up the gross neglect. He put his hand up.

"Mr. Sherman?" said the unsuspecting Principal.

"Just a few thoughts," he would say. "I know we could all be threatened with more parent involvement for this, but I say the school is too big, too diverse! I say we do not need 2400 savages on one street-corner every day. Society is afraid to have more than a dozen of them together anywhere else. Here we are, un-armed, with 2400 of them. And they hate each other and mock each other—try to injure or maim, rape or kill, or just gross each other out. All of the problems of all of the world are represented here in this building. I say we separate them: a school for the gifted, a school for the above average, a school for the new kid in the country, a school for the IRA, a school for the PLO—and one for the twisted, the perverted, the insane, and the just plain rotten little sons of..."

"Thank you, Mr. Sherman. we'll get right on that."

"And you need one for the immature: the kid who is

fine, except for the fact that he's developing slowly. No reason a pink-faced boy should have to go to school and sit next to a kid with a beard and too much body hair; no reason a flat-chested little virgin should have to go to school with a savvy street slut with three kids. There are little boys and little girls who just want to nudge and giggle but are already in high school . . ."

"Uh . . . security? Will you please wrap Mr. Sherman in something soft and pillowy and take him to my office . . ."

It would be like that. Probably. It wasn't that they were closed to new ideas; they just had no appreciation of the fine points, the nuances of . . . of . . . sleep deprivation. He was so groggy . . .

Mr. Sherman was on his stomach slithering along the floor in the main hallway by the boys' restroom. Suddenly, right before him but unaware, the Iranian kid. Stealthily, he moved closer, behind the kid. And then, like a cobra, he rose up, and, with frightening speed, struck. The kid's entire spinal column crumbled into white powder and ran out the left leg of his blue jeans. Sherm tossed the lifeless, powdery sack to the floor, and turned away, a wry smile on his crooked lips. A rabid mob of villagers, attacking now with pitchforks and other farm tools, moved in, screaming. Nothing could touch him if he could just stand by his door. It was written somewhere.

He ran and ran. He counted 2399 kids as he ran through the building. Only the Iranian kid down there on the floor was missing. Then, at last, he was safe at his door. A temporary calm fell over his soul, but only for an instant. Velma floated toward him on a cloud of pink mist, in slow motion, sensuously, writhingly, lookin' good. He could feel his ears turning red, and he could feel the eyes of his disappointed colleagues looking at him, burning into him. But, he said, "What the hell!" And he grabbed Velma and gathered her into his arms and hugged the living soup out of her—drawing her young perfect face up closer to his wrinkled gray joke, and he promptly snapped her neck just short of kissing her violently and passionately like Woody Allen. But he dropped her to the floor right there by his door.

Because inside, in the back of his classroom, in his isolated desk, Jerome was on fire! He was burning up back there—silently—not saying a word. He didn't even have his hand up. He was just blazing merrily away, and Mr. Sherman had to save him because Mr. Sherman was Jerome's idol! But the room was full of papers—ungraded, slippery, slimy piles of papers. The desks were spewing them into the aisles, whole bundles of them with rubber bands; piles of them were falling like towers from both sides as he tried to get to Jerome; walls of papers grew from the floor; it rained papers. It was Mardi Gras, Times Square, a ticker-tape parade/avalanche. And Jerome sat there burning. "Charge, you sorry-assed recruit! Marines never leave a man behind!" The colonel barked at him from behind him somewhere. "Gung Ho! Semper Fi! You pathetic piece of . . ." But Mr. Sherman slipped, fell, flailed, crawled, wriggled, clammored, finally began swimming toward the flames—and drowning, then sinking into the flaming papers, the rotting, reeking, ungraded fire hazards.

It took the Regulator clock with the screwed-up hands to scatter that one. Mr. Sherman came off the couch, his arms plying the air of the dark living room; and then, composure.

He looked around for his wife. She always hated it when he woke up flailing and/or screaming. Post-Teaching Stress Syndrome: not as bad as soldiers have, but bad enough. He tried to imagine what it would be like to have survived both combat and teaching. Or *had* he survived?

He had lost his little hat, and the serape was twisted. But he was calm. He was fine. Really.

To the sliding glass door now, and another look at the blizzard—and, indeed, he would call it a blizzard now—very satisfying. He thought of the thousands of students and dozens of teachers who would be watching for the name of their school among the closings announced on TV—lucky people who would, instead of sallying forth in the morning, just roll over and turn out the light. And how he wanted to just let go, right now, and come back to the therapy another night—possibly all other nights. But the snow needed to be watched, and Mr. Sherman needed to feel the slow release of care that came with the overpowering grip of the accumulating snow.

Another kind of day was possible: the kind when only those who can get to school must attend. No bus service. The valiant attempts by teacher and student to get to school on such days and keep the place technically open in the eyes of the state: that was Mr. Sherman—always had been! The more he thought about it, the truer it was: he would wade the deep snow, plow his way through anything to get to school—always. He remembered playing a game at noontime in Minnesota—to see who could stay outside longest in the blast. And School Patrol, and raising the flag in the morning—that was Mr. Sherman out there in the snow, always. If they opened up the building, he was there. And now he loved the snow because it closed that school. Go figure.

"You know what? I'm sensing conflict again!"

"Shut up."

"Seriously, Mr. Sherman. Think about it. You don't just want snow, you want cataclysmic snow—paralyzing and dangerous. So that there will be no school. But you loved school. What's up with that?'

"It's you again, isn't it?" said Mr. Sherman, turning toward the recliner.

"All hail!" said Shakespeare, rather sarcastically.

"I don't know. Part of the fun of school is the day when there's no school. Does that make sense?"

"Thou must leave off of this, elst thou wilt go mad."

"Get off it! I'm okay here. Okay, I'm up in the night having a conversation with a dead guy. And I have moved out here where there are no people, to get away from people, and I've been alone too long. Okay. I'm out here really missing teaching, yet very happy that I'm not doing it anymore. I complain that, by being a teacher, I gave up other things, like war, addiction, free love, hard physical work, Woodstock. I missed everything, and now I've come out here to get away from it all . . . I know that." His voice trailed off.

"A tale, told by an idiot, full of sound and fury, signifying nothing?"

"Something like that. That was a good line."

"Wasn't it!? Damn! I think so, too. Proceed."

"Proceed? There is no 'proceed' here, dammit. I'm through with it. I've got my Id out playing with it here in front of someone who isn't even there—and may have been an elaborate hoax to begin with."

"Ah, but there are the plays! How says't thou?"

"Yeah. The plays. The body of works is more important than the author."

"Or authors?"

"Look, I'm confused enough here. Let's not go into that. This is MY nightmare, and I have a lot at stake."

"Aye. Sanity by sunrise. A noble goal."

He looked at the Regulator clock. Wee small hours. It seemed he had a long way to go, and not enough time. But he was grateful to be doing this embarrassing stuff in private. This truly must never see the light of day.

Not everyone was this lucky. It took no effort at all to think of an example. It was Fourth Lunch—a half-hour impacted heavily by large numbers of kids trying to get fed, sometimes having missed an earlier opportunity because of a test or an emergency. Anyway, the landscape was fuzzy with people, and Mr. Sherman inadvertently stumbled into one of the programed horrors of school. A large donut of students had formed in an area adjacent to the main lunch room: always an indication of a fight or similar spectacle. The donut is usually impenetrable, but foolishly he plunged into it and broke into the inner circle.

There on the floor, a half-clothed girl was seizing and screaming and vomiting, having lost control of both her bowels and her bladder. She had torn out large swatches of her hair; she was bleeding; she was exposed. Some of the students were laughing, some crying, some trying to help, some trying to leave, some nearly hysterical. Other teachers and the nurse somehow broke through behind Mr. Sherman, and the girl was subdued and covered and the kids driven away in all directions. Everyone knew the girl: she was a Special Ed kid who had been mainstreamed into the regular student body. The rules seemed to be the same for her as for the dyslexic kid, or the A.D.D. kid, or the Mongoloid kid.

"We are proud of Mainstreaming," he remembered someone saying at an In-Service. "It is good for everyone: the special students, the teachers, and the main student body. The occasional disruption is acceptable."

That particular disruption was probably a part of the nightmares of many of those who were there to witness it, especially the poor kid in the middle of the donut. A rare case—just not rare enough. Mr. Sherman concluded that he could have gone all through his life without that experience and been just fine: a selfish, non-scientific view, perhaps, but this was school, not hospital, and kids, not interns.

In timber country, they call something like this a "controlled burn." Mr. Sherman had been fascinated with that term because of the little paradox. Still, we control fire all the time. His wife would call the sheriff's office and report a forest fire twenty miles away, off down the valley in "the view"—the expanse visible in the daytime from what was the black window this night. The sheriff's people would assure her that it was just a controlled burn. It meant that forest debris, useless undergrowth, dead things mainly, were being burned and transformed into nutrients for the growing forest. The big trees were not burning.

Well! Mr. Sherman knew a metaphor when he saw one! This was exactly what Mr. Sherman was attempting here: he was trying to "burn off" all the dead stuff, the superfluous debris of his past—dangerous tinder that could accidentally ignite and consume him. Damn! Not bad! Stuff like Jerome and the Iranian kid, Velma and the faculty meetings and assessments, all the injustices and abuses—dry debris, irrelevant now, but still there. Better off ashes! Let 'em burn.

But, whereas a controlled burn lets in the light and air, creates fertile ground, new life and growth, there is an element of risk. "Calculated risk" was another fun expression. And Mr. Sherman had never been much of a risk taker. Getting out his night devils and playing with them, deliberately fighting with them—this had never been his style. It had happened accidentally in the past: lots of little wild fires. But he had never before pressed his luck.

And he felt lucky, really. He had never been what could be considered unlucky. Late in 1939, while the Germans were stomping through Poland, Mr. Sherman was born—too young for World War II, too young for Korea. When Viet Nam blew, he found himself beyond reach. "I stayed in class and saved my ass," someone said. He did not walk up and volunteer, but he lived with his One-A rating, played the Viet Nam lottery, and was deferred or just a bit old by the time things got critical, and he missed the war—somehow. He never went into the streets with a misspelled sign; he never went to Canada—could not have done that; but he hated everything about that war and was happy to miss it. Guilt, gratitude, but no scars.

His 'war' had been in the classroom. Once, he had tried the real world: the one out there where people do lunch, live on phone calls, commute, work nine-to-five, go to the john when they have to, and don't have to break up fights. But it was no good. He was back in the classroom in six months. Whenever he felt like a coward, he thought of the millions of people who would rather donate an organ than face an audience. He had fought all of his battles in the classroom—or near his door.

"Damn. I suppose it is inevitable: rationalizing again, and trying to give honor and dignity to mere teaching."

"Y'all jist a little bitty ol' piss-ant teacher, Boy! Y'all woulda got money if y'all wuz important! 'Member that. Y'all suppose to git yer pay in the form of warm fuzzy experiences—and, of course, crystal apples! Git a grip, Boy!"

Warm fuzzies! Mr. Sherman checked the snowstorm to make sure it was still running properly, checked the clock, referred to The Plan. There was still time to drag out the warm fuzzy stories—the dozens and dozens of heart-rending Hallmark commercials—the tear-jerkers, the three-hanky jobs that make it all worth it: stories about saving endangered ghetto children from their environments—about letting the bedraggled dog into the school out of the rain—about filling in for the absent father off to war—about helping the child cope with bullies. A little violin music, perhaps.

It was payback time. He could collect now if he could come up with a warm fuzzy tale from his rich career.

Well, there was the time when he got a "See Me" note in his mailbox—from the principal. It was a male principal that time, before the whole thing became a matriarchy. The note could mean something serious, or it could be friendly: he could be fired or bronzed or get a crystal apple. It could go either way. He approached with trepidation.

"Good afternoon, Mr. Sherman. Sit down a minute—gotta share something with you." It sounded friendly enough.

"Thank you."

"How'd things go today?" Uh-oh, could be bad.

"Okay. No biggies that I noticed. Seemed to go smoothly."

"Good. Yesterday . . ."

"Yesterday?"

"Yesterday, they were giving blood in the room next to yours, is that right?'

"Yeah. 116. Now, that was a circus!"

"And your door was open?"

"Yeah. We were doing a little free writing. No formal presentation going on . . ."

"How many kids came into your class and fainted?"

"Oh, I think it was about three, maybe four for all-day."

"Three or four. Do you remember a Miss uh . . ." He consulted an ominous-looking slip of paper. "Miss Sally James?"

"One guy and about three girls. I knew two of the kids, but, no—I don't know Sally James."

"Well, according to this, she staggered into your room and fainted, and you caught her and lowered her to the floor."

"Yeah. It was like that all day. We got her feet up—well, all of them, really—elevated their feet and called the medical people in from next door. All day long."

"Well, Mr. Sherman, I am happy to inform you that Sally's mother, Mrs. Elmer James, has decided not to sue you."

"Me? Sue me? Well, good! My God."

"We were able to talk her out of it. We conviced her that you were just trying to help. Of course, her lawyer . . ."

"Lawyer! My God—they had a lawyer on this?"

"There's always a lawyer in there somewhere," the principal said dryly. "But ours was here, too, and we got it stopped."

"But, what . . . ? What did I do? What were they . . . ?"

"Girl said she was humiliated—exposed."

"Oh. That was the kid with the short skirt!"

"Yep. Spent half the afternoon lying in that room giving blood and recovering and drinking orange juice, and then your room and fainting and getting all pale and all that—all that with a short skirt. Probably a dress-code violation, possibly fire-code—God knows what."

"Anyway, she's not suing?"

"Not you. May sue the school, the blood people, and possibly the manufacturers of the skirt. But you are not included. Just thought you would like to know, just in case . . ."

"In case?"

"Yeah: in case the story gets out."

Mr. Sherman remembered how warm and fuzzy he had felt—how not being sued had made his day. Even now, years later, there was a lump in his throat. And he remembered how, thereafter and forevermore he had resolved to catch fainting female students on first bounce.

But certainly, there must have been a warmer story in all the years at Hugh Stone High. Well, there was the day when LOTS of kids fainted in his room. They were trying to sign up for his English class. He was so popular that they would fight over his class. Either that, or they were trying to avoid Mrs. Maxon, another English teacher, who flunked everyone who was pretty or black or Oriental or Mexican or Jewish or dumb . . . well, you get the idea. She was tough. She had also taught Herbert Hoover. Anyway, the kids had mobbed his room, broken down the barrier at his door, flooded inside, sucked all the air out of the place, and begun fainting en masse. Mr. Sherman had been treed atop a drafting table at the back of the room, and all of the sign-up sheets had been destroyed. Now THAT was heart-warming. Such popularity! Absolutely gratifying! Better than money! (Well, maybe not better than money . . .) The floor ended up knee-deep in fallen kids.

That was the end of "running for classes"—the way it was done before the computer. It took a few days to get it all straightened out, and, although it was flattering, it was also frightening. But nobody died, so it was warm and fuzzy. Or, not.

There just had to be better stuff. A letter? A valentine? Sure. Lots of that all the time. Commonplace, really. The kids had liked Mr. Sherman and said so—behaved generally well, and let him teach. So the kids were off the hook, really.

And then, just like that, it hit him: Of course there was a heart-warming story! Mr. Sherman shut his eyes—just for a moment—over by the sliding glass door—and he remembered.

It was nearly Christmas, and the mercury had plunged into the upper eighties. Old Hugh Stone High was about to dismiss for the holiday vacation—two weeks! The mood was incredible. There were no decorations or Christmas trees because of the fire code and the separation of church and state, but it was Christmas. The kids had been wild all week, but no shots were fired; some tires were missing in the parking lot, but the cars were still there; it was near poetry. Gifts had been smuggled in all week; exchanges had occured, teachers looking the other way. Many kids had saved some dope money and bought Christmas gifts instead.

As they went out the main doors and burst into freedom, kids would scream, "Merry *&%$#in' Christmas, you *&¢%$#@in' #$¢&s!" It was their way. Or they would say, "See you in *&¢%$#$@in' January; hope Santa &¢%$#in' Claus brings you some *&¢%$#in' good ¢%$#@%!" The spirit of the season permeated the whole escape sequence.

It was then that Mr. Sherman found the poor little Freshman girl sitting on the floor in the hallway by her locker, crying like her heart was broken. "She no doubt has no place to go for Christmas," he mused. "Probably has no presents to give her loved ones—or maybe she's from a broken home: mom, dad, dad's girlfriend—the usual story. Poor kid."

He approached the child quietly. "Can I help you, young lady?"

"Oh just *&¢$# off! You don't know me!"

"You seem to be having trouble here. I may be able to help. Do you need transportation? Food? Clothing? Money?"

"I said, *&¢%¢$# off! I don't need some #%¢&&$%in' geeze in my face! Just leave me the %¢$#%@ alone!"

"But you are crying! And it's Christmas!"

"Like, what part of '&¢%$#$ off' is it that you don't understand, you old %$&¢%$#!? Is it the '&¢%$#%¢' or the 'off'?"

Mr. Sherman was beginning to sense conflict—and said so. Another teacher came along, and then another.

"Would all you &¢%$#@in' old &¢%$¢&s just take a *&¢%$#in' hike? Jesus Christ!"

"But, you're crying!"

"I can't get my *&¢%$#in' locker open," she said finally—but only after Mr. Deeton neared the area. "It's ¢%$#@&in' jammed or some &¢%$# thing!"

Mr. Sherman walked over and hit the locker door with the butt of his hand, and the door opened, and someone's Christmas was saved. From what he could see, all of this little girl's friends would be getting little baggies of pungent-smelling brownies for Christmas. He had saved the day.

And, as he was about to walk away, he heard the child call after him, "Oh . . . uh . . . Old Dude? Thanks for the *&¢%$#in' help, Man. And Merry Christmas." Chicken soup for the *&¢%$in' soul!

Sometimes it's like that: all happiness and warm puppies, tiny fingers plucking at the heartstrings. How he missed it all.

And such language. He imagined Ol' Minnie Mae—Dr. Minnie Mae—coming up with a test that would communicate with the current generation. Question: Like, who the *&¢%$# discovered ¢%$#%¢in' America? Answer: Christopher &¢%$#@in' Columbus, Dude!

Hide and watch.

Chapter Ten

Mr. Sherman was being dragged through a dark gauntlet of spinning columns of fetid, flailing ragged mops, slashing and slapping from above, below, back, front, and sides; he was being jammed through a chaotic hullabaloo of screams and cries, maniacal laughter, groans, and howls, punctuated by deafening metallic bangs; he was being propelled—shoved—stuffed into a mealstrom of smoke and sweat, dank musk and fear and antiseptic—and sucked into a kaleidoscope of leering faces, pierced and maimed, tattooed and painted and scarred; he was being pummeled and hammered by bug-eyed, grinning imps and fiends—assailed by a hellish roaring barrage of projectiles, flying elbows, stenches, nauseating tastes, and disturbing auras. No doubt about it: Mr. Sherman had blundered into the Freshman wing of the old building at Hugh Stone High. The bell had rung.

Probably an accident, even within a nightmare. The old building was a morass of rampant puberty from which he had been delivered in the later years; yet, in an ill-selected nightmare now and then since retirement, he had found himself trapped there at bell time in that hallway, or, worse, inside a cascade of nudging, plucking, buffeting hellions in a urine-soaked stairwell.

Still, there was a Coke machine in a faculty lounge over there, and it was possible to mistime things.

Mr. Sherman shuddered and took another sip of Diet Coke. Plasma. "There was nothing insane about getting out of *there*," he concluded. He noticed that he was sweating again.

It was cooling to look out at the snow, though. He stood by his door again and squinted for a peek at Miss Whitby out there turning into a lurid ice sculpture. It was almost certainly Miss Whitby and her Salvation Army Thrift Shop grocery cart—piled high in places now, still recognizable, but less distinct than before—softening, rounding over. He imagined her over there in The Old Building with the Freshmen at bell time—with her rickety stolen grocery cart with its stubborn wheels, nearly square toward the end there—the clamor, the obscene jeering: Miss Whitby's teaching career.

By dawn it would be a lump of snow. Period.

"You can't save them all," he heard someone babbling.

"Whee. Cliché time. But did I save any of them?" he muttered to whoever it was.

"Now, Mr. Sherman, you and I agreed a long time ago—over Margaritas, so it was official—that we would probably both get into Heaven, if they go on having Heaven." Jerry opened his hand and did that down-stroke on the facial foilage. "We agreed that we 'fought the good fight'—right there in the front lines: right in the big middle of integration, immigration, socialization, maturation, naturalization . . ."

"Christmas Vacation, Summer Vacation . . ."

"We agreed—over Margaritas, now!—that we had fought in the front lines, long and valiantly. We had touched humanity, molded young minds, won the worship in their eyes. We had done well. Now you retire, and you come back here for a perfectly good Friday meeting, and you doubt your sainthood? I am ashamed of you!"

Yeah. There had been such a meeting. Mr. Sherman had thrown down his hammers and trowels, unplugged his sanders, saws and drills, and holstered his screwdrivers, and headed for the city for a bit of nostalgia.

And there was something in Jerry's voice that was deadly serious. It was clear that failure at retirement was not going to be tolerated.

"I don't know: you get out there, and you look back, and you wonder if you ever did anybody any good."

"You need more Margaritas on that mountain of yours."

"More? There are no Margaritas out there. Could be."

"Maybe it's the fresh air," offered Darby. "I've heard that a sudden reduction of methane, propane, and carbon dioxide can muddle the thought processes."

"Maybe I'm star happy. I had forgotten about the stars, but they're still out there. No, it's the Margaritas—or maybe just the salt. I don't know if I've ever mentioned it, but . . ."

"You don't really like Margaritas, it's the salt. Right." Colleen reminded him that these friends had talked a lot of things over for a long time.

"But *you* have saved souls, done good deeds. I've watched you!"

"We all save kids, Mr. Sherman. I'm sticking with the original declaration." Jerry hoisted his Margarita.

"And you are out there doing what we all want to do: go off somewhere and brood about it. It's good for you. I fully intend to go to an abandoned monastery off the Irish coast and brood when I retire—for 15 minutes. It's colder than a principal's heart out there." Colleen knew about such places.

"That's the bad thing: I've put in more than 15 minutes."

"Well, quit that! You've done it—you're outa here. Nobody is cutting on your carcass; you are not on fire; you are not poor. Enjoy, already!"

"You are right. Life is good."

"So tell us about Bambi and Thumper and the wild turkeys. Tell us about the armadillos and the errant emu. Just don't tell us not to retire!" Darby was actually attempting a beer at this meeting.

"The main thing that you will notice is that there seems to be a way to win—once you disengage, I mean. You spring free of conflicting expectations, Catch 22's, treadmill futility, piles of papers. It's great!"

"Oh shut up and drink your Margarita. You look ten years younger, so shut up. You don't have to get up early. Shut up."

"I'm shutting up: right here and now, in this noble emporium of spirited if not spiritual delights—here in this sacred, calm, dark, secure island of respite . . ."

All together: "Shut up!"

"Did I mention that I had jury duty and didn't grade papers in court?"

All together: "Shut up!"

For some reason, they didn't wanna hear about it. At least that was the impression Mr. Sherman got. Darn. Go figure!

Nobody was lurking in the recliner when he brought his mind back to the present and focused. When he had been unable to sleep anywhere else, always he had been able to kick back in that old recliner and nod off. Now, he reasoned, if he went over there and sat down—and how it beckoned!—the vigil would be over.. He was not certain that it was working anyway, this all-nighter; yet, he had faced many of the thorny patches in the swamps of his past, and he at least *felt* sane. A sour stomach, maybe, and some post nasal drip, but sane—at least not raving, rabid madness. The recliner would challenge, but it would comfort, too.

He sat, eased back, contemplated the still ceiling fan for

a moment, then engaged the wooden lever on the side of the chair, dropped the thing back into its stretch position, and locked it into a sprawl. And he began to melt. To hell with all of it.

"Sit sit sit! Welcome everyone. Our In-Service Workshop this afternoon is entitled 'Empowerment Through Cringing Obedience.' Can you say, 'Cringing Obedience'?"

Nausea of buttermilk proportions hit Mr. Sherman in a disgusting hot wave. He clawed at the air, thrashed away with arms and legs, trapped there in the chair like a roach on its back. Somehow, he hit the lever and released the spine of the thing, pulled with his thighs, and managed to free himself. He flung himself at the sliding glass door, yanked it aside, and hurled everything he had eaten in recent memory out into the storm.

The storm flung snow back at him, and an especially large glob of it rose from the railing and hit him full in the face. He fired another broadside, summoning up unremembered and unrecognizable trash, further sullying the deck. More snow flew back at him, and then he felt himself reaching way back, down deep. His final volley included ancient chalk dust, pencil sharpener debris, red pencils, Post-Its, Xeroxed memos, even Ditto fluid and crayons. The ultimate purge!

He stood there barefooted and gasping, trembling and temporarily confused, but not stupid and not crazy. The long-awaited storm was sincere. He staggered back inside and shut the door, saving the carpet twice in minutes. Would Wifey notice?

And then he noticed a discomfort in his left eye. Some object that did not belong there was definitely there! In a moment he had rubbed a curious fragment out of the eye: something obviously dislodged by the strain of vomiting.

It was not a mystery. Nothing was a mystery anymore.

Now he knew the filthy truth, a truth that had been kept from him by this very object.

It was an implant designed to block his memory of certain events. But it had gone awry this night with this sudden nausea. Oh, he knew what it was, all right! He had seen this on satellite TV. Anybody would know what this thing was. We are probably full of implants The Bastards have crammed into us in the dead of night.

He knew, and he remembered now: the bright light overhead that night in the city, right in his own back yard—the ray of white light that had snatched him from his own back yard, and pulled him up into "some sort of ship." He had found himself helpless on his back on a strange table in a place that seemed near and familiar, yet unearthly and foreign, which kinda figures. And he had been obscenely probed, he could now remember, and very personally examined by beings he could not recognize as human. Colorless wires had been hooked to his extremities—all of his extremities, including the one you don't want any wires hooked to. (Damned prepositions.) He remembered pain and humiliation and revulsion, and a slight draft.

He had been determined to give them nothing, whoever they were. Whatever they wanted, he would not cooperate. He fought them with everything he had, because it seemed important at the time. But they did not need his words. The little electrodes would tell all.

Nearby he remembered seeing a sort of guage—like a thermometer, but hooked also to a digital presentation, like on the new oven Mr. Sherman had installed in the kitchen. It was hooked to the colorless wires, and he wondered if what flowed through the wires went two ways.

And then the torture: "Lunch Duty!" a voice said, and the meter hit nine! "Monday Morning" the voice said, sleepily. The guage read 8.5. He understood the machine now, but it was too late. "Parent Conference," said the voice, and that was a ten—with lights and sirens, claxons, even ooogah horns, and strobes.

There was apparently nothing he could do. “Mainstreaming” brought a 9.7, despite his efforts to block the response. It went on and on like that: “Stand by your door,” then “PTA Meeting” and “See Me.” “Dr. Spock” rated right up there with “Hall Duty” and “Open Fly in Class.” It was horrible, and now he could remember it all.

Mr. Sherman had spilled his guts to whoever they were. He had betrayed his fellow teachers and given weapons to the enemy. Everything teachers hate most was now in the data banks of the enemy. “Fire Drill,” the voice slashed! and “babysitter”—they got it all. He was roundly raped, body and soul and mind. Somewhere, echoing, far away, he heard strains of “Dueling Banjos.”

This was how they did it, then. They knew where he was all the time, and they could drop little slop-filled balloons on his head at any time. Like buttermilk. None of it had been an accident. Deep inside, he had suspected this all along.

How many others had they gathered up, plugged in, and drained of secret information? How many others had been perfectly and precisely targeted because of this abduction routine?

It was too much. He took the implant on his fingertip and tried to put it back—back into his eye. He had remembered quite enough! He needed to re-block his memory. But which eye? And How? The anguish, overwhelming responsibility, the humiliation of having been the rat who armed the enemy was too much!

And then, he dropped the implant. On his knees on the carpet, he crawled about, raking with his fingertips, searching, hopeless. He finally fell to the floor and wept.

“Accountability,” the voice chided. “Ebonics!” “Mission Statement!” “Walk the walk; talk the talk!” He writhed and retched—twitched with each added blow.

"John Dewey" "Bloom!" "Modifications." "Vouchers." "Outcome Based Education!" Would it never end? Each word struck like a bullet. Mr. Sherman seriously considered prayer, surrender, escape, union action, letters to Congress, Oprah.

They knew about all of it, and nothing could be done. He remembered, he was pretty sure. The implant was now part of Wifey's Oriental carpet, or their new hardwood floor.

Someday they would get him. It would be Ol' Billy Joe Jim Bob Willie Wayne Kline's turn to be on the carpet—a tenuous thought transition, but Mr. Sherman was still crazy!

"Are you now, or have you ever been a little green man?" asked Senator Thompson—or he almost certainly would ask the question if a congressional investigation ever came down. And, if alien abduction talk were ever linked to the sabotage of American Public Education, Congress would have to hold hearings. It is written.

"Ah cain't hep y'all, Senator. Muh sleeze-bag attorney says to take the Fifth all the way," Ol' Billy Joe et cetera would say.

Then Senator Kennedy would jump in. "I should like to uh . . . point out that uh . . . this is not a court of law," he would offer. "We are striving to find thee uh facts. Thee uh Fifth Amendment does not apply."

"Lemme talk tuh this peckerwood," Senator Thurmond would drawl. "Ah kin honor stain 'im and git 'im talkin'. Ah got tuh Ol' Benedict Arnold, and Ah'll git tuh this sorry piece o' . . ."

But he would fall asleep about there, or lose interest. Other questions would come, however:

"Is it true that unspeakable acts were performed upon kidnapped teachers in an effort to discover their likes and dis-likes? Is it true that the information elicited through torture was used to annoy, exacerbate, and generally piss off all of teacherkind?"

"Ah cain't recall . . ."

"Lemme cut this peckerwood!"

"And is it true that flattery, promises, and crystal apples were used in lieu of money?"

"Son, them teachers luv them crystal apples, so hush yo' mouth!"

"Is uh this why you attached electrodes to their..uh..dangling participles?" Ol' Kennedy would kick some butt.

"Ah have no recollection . . ."

"Sir, is it not true that you head up a clandestine Think Tank that deliberately concocts, coordinates, and conducts dirty, rotten, sneaky policies . . . ?"

"No comment."

But Thompson would persist. "Did you or did you not use the computer to deceive The Press and to squeeze money out of the government—and then use the money for something else entirely?"

"Everybody duz that."

"Have you conspired with standardized testing agencies of opposing philosophies to extract money from the public? Have you asked our children to think without first providing a language of thought—to express ideas without a vocabulary or structure—to compose without a fact base?"

"Hell, that's just Progressive Education."

"Did you conspire to blame the public school and its innocent teachers for racism, communism, drug addiction, crime, epidemics . . ."

"Not really."

"Then why did you ask them to cure these ailments?"

"Ah cannot recall."

"Did you not mandate a never-ending cycle of reform,

acceleration, remediation, generalization, specialization, mutation, and random alteration?"

"Excuse me?"

"Along with re-tooled buzz words and obscurist rhetoric . . ."

"No comment."

"For the purpose of encumbering the educational processes to the point of gridlock?"

"Jist Standard Operational Procedure, Senator."

"Did you set us up? The whole country?"

"On the advice o' muh smarmy, reeking, low-life lawyer, Ah respectfully decline . . ."

"Y'all, Suh, are the Devil, and ahmo cutcha!"

Then maybe they would let Ol' Strom cut him!

Oh, they would pin Ol' Billy Joe et cetera to the wall, make no mistake. If the Senate didn't, the House would. But it would probably be the Senate. Look what they did to Julius Ceasar—stabbed the living soup out of him. Read your Shakespeare, Man. Thirty-three wounds, all oozing blessed juices and dagger drippings. Mr. Sherman had faith that Ol' Billy Joe would get his—eventually.

Okay, it was the middle of the night and he was having anachronisms again, or just mixing literature with history. He did not care whose Senate got the bastard, just so the bastard got got! (All semblences of grammar had left Mr. Sherman's body, probably with the vomit, into the storm somewhere, all puce and kiwi and cranberry and mango-colored, and frozen in the snow.)

He awoke there on the carpet. So, maybe the abduction was a little iffy. But why not? Damn near three million people say they're abducted on a regular basis—and probed. It would explain a lot. Maybe it was all more complicated than alien abduction, a Think Tank conspiracy, or just money. But Mr.

Sherman had been part of something sinister and very bad for his country for over thirty years. But what?

He vowed to think deeper—just as soon as he summoned the strength to get off the floor.

Almost invariably, however, things had been much simpler than Mr. Sherman imagined. At least, others had found things less complicated. He noticed that none of his friends had a mysterious person following them and moving their car when they shopped at WalMart. But that was like the thing in the garage, too—and the Think Tank. It was real, and it was personal.

"Mr. Sherman, you disappoint me."

"Well, of course I do, Jerry. It's what I do."

"I mean, here you are all knotted up about mentoring your Miss Whitby, and it's all so simple!"

"I know. That's what I keep hearing. Simple."

"Well, Duh!" said Colleen. "How complicated can this be? Just set her down and explain the whole structure of Good Old Hugh Stone High."

"Yeah. Tell her the rules," Darby tossed in. And then she unveiled The Grin. There was a brief silence so that it would all register with Mr. Sherman, and then he realized that this was a set-up. He had crossed the line again, and the gang was going to straighten him out.

"Mr. Sherman," said Jerry, "your friends have decided to help you mentor Miss Whitby up one side and down the other, forever and ever, world without end—so that Fridays can be brighter."

"I need all the help I can get. Let's order more Margaritas."

For just a moment, it looked serious, Mr. Sherman remembered. But then Jerry spoke. "You have to explain The System to her. Miss Whitby has to understand that The District is so large that it is divided into Areas I, II, III, IV, and V, that each area has elementary, middle, and high schools, and 'special' schools for total sociopaths. And Hugh Stone High is a school with Freshmen, Sophomores, Juniors and Seniors; 9th, 10th, 11th, and 12th graders." Jerry loved stuff like this.

"But you have to tell her that it's so big that it has to be cut up into House I, House II, House III, and House IV—each one of which has kids from grades 9, 10, 11, and 12. And each House has a full load of bureaucrats and offices."

"And rules," said Darby, "and secretaries."

"Thank you, my friends. I can see where this is going."

"Each kiddo," said Jerry, "is brown, yellow, black, or white—catholic, protestant, Jewish, or undecided.'

"But deciding,' said Colleen. "Each kid is an adolescent, trying to figure out what he is: masculine, feminine, neuter, undecided—and how he learns: visually, hands-on, through sound or smell, from books or whatever—straight out of Ed. 101 back in college. It's all true."

"Tell her that. And about their interests: science, math, music, art, literature, speech, drama, auto mechanics, history, foreign language—real world or virtual reality . . ."

"Old wing or new wing, first, second or Third floor—major works, remedial, or regular—A.D.H.D., E.D., etc."

"Yeah. C.O.D., D.O.A., puce, kiwi, cranberry . . ."

"Democrat, Republican, or Independent—Hispanic, Oriental, African. Half-empty or half-full. Type A or Type B. X chromosomes or Y—or why not? Leo, Virgo, Ram, Gemini? Anorexic. Atheletic. Intellectual. Both. All. None. Chess player or non-chess player. Keep it simple."

"Yeah. Simple. Just tell her it's all real simple, and that she will have hundreds of individuals who are all of these things and more. No sweat, Mr. Sherman. Clue her in."

"Right. I'll just tell her to wheel her grocery cart right

down the middle."

"Sure. It's high school: gay, straight, AC/DC, tall, short, undecided and hating it . . ."

"Growing. Stunted. Big accouterments, small accouterments, egotistical with no reason, self-destructive, self-sympathetic, just pathetic . . ."

"Just tell her she's a big sister, surrogate parent, counselor, friend, role model, guru, saint, sage and five-foot authority figure with her own stolen grocery cart. Hell, tell her she's a mentor!"

"Thank you, my friends."

"You wanna write this all down on some butcher paper? I have a Magic Marker in my purse—rolled up in the rule book."

"Never mind."

"Drivers, non-drivers, bus kids, free lunch, brown-baggers, geniuses, idiots, maniacs, phobiacs, addicts, pushers, smitten, sane, Communists, Buddhists, dreamers, anal retentives, nerds, geeks, rich, poor . . ."

"Jerry."

"Pretty, plain, dyslexic, myopic, bald, pierced . . ."

"Jerry!"

"Bantu, Zulu, Mandarin, Siamese, Ceylonese, Formosan, Choctaw, Cree, Crow, Ute . . ."

"Jerry, I get it! And you're dating yourself! We don't even have some of those things anymore."

"Bring her to a Margarita meeting! *We'll* mentor her until she screams."

"There might be a rule against mentors and mentees and Margaritas. I'll look it up."

"Estonians, Yugoslavians, Transylvanians, Yankees, Dodgers, stalkers, voyeurs, religious fanatics, soap opera freaks, Cheerleaders, crybabies . . ."

"Yes, yes, I'll fill her in."

"And be sure to show her our Mission Statement!

Especially the part about World Peace. And the rule about standing by your door."

"She doesn't have a door. She doesn't have a room."

"Tell her she'll have to stand by her cart—and be a referee, a peace keeper, a beat cop, an inspiration. She should probably clean and polish her cart daily. There's got to be a rule about that. I'll look it up."

'Thank you, Darby. Thank you all. If we weren't on the first floor, I would jump out the window."

"I propose a toast to Miss Whitby—an Irish toast." All raised their glasses. "May the hallway rise before her; may the wheels on her grocery cart remain firm and round; and may she get a room of her own before The Bastards drive her out!"

"Amen."

"Fetishists and numismatists, scuba-divers and pom-pom girls, Dow and Nasdaq, epistemologists and typists . . ."

"Good Grief, Jerry!"

"That, too."

Bulletin: Teachers are not to allow guns or gunfire in class until further notice.

Chapter Eleven

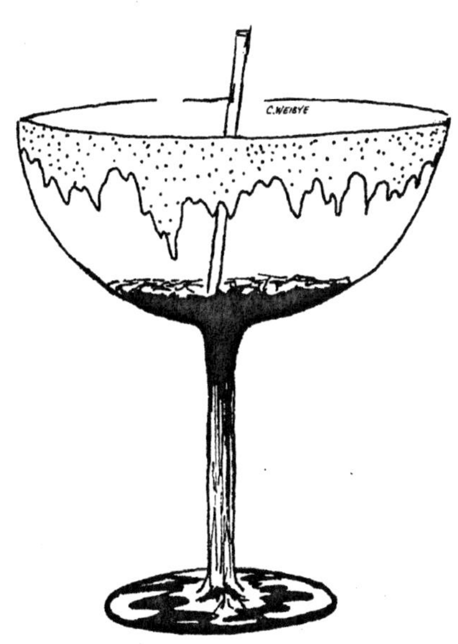

Oh, she was still out there, all right: a lump now, almost covered, but still there. All he could see was Miss Whitby's eyes, cursing him. The grocery cart could have been anything—anything grotesque and haunted. But her eyes!

And he *had* mentored, dammit! Actually, he had mentored the living soup out of Miss Whitby, now that he really thought about it.

She had come to him one afternoon, without her grocery cart. He had known her anyway. And she had been around long enough by that time to be full of questions. And he had answered. Willingly.

"There are little groups of teachers all over the parking lot. They talk earnestly, then look at the school. What's up with that?"

"Elementary, my child. Come: let me mentor you. These are political times—very sensitive political times. And what you are seeing in the faculty parking lot is the caucus process. These meetings are the most important ones the teachers have." Together they had stepped to a window. "Notice that a small group of black teachers is huddled over there by the large sedan. Nearby, a mixed group by the Volkswagen. Further out, by my van, a white group. This means that the meetings are about money!"

"How do you know they're talking about money?"

"Because I'm supposed to be out there by my van! Today's topic is the large treasure-trove just dropped on us from Washington. They're going to put in a whole new layer of administrators with it."

"How do you know that?"

"See the black group? Well, Al got the word from his sister-in-law who works downtown that the money is going for more assistant vice principals. That's what happened to the room that would have been yours."

"My room! They gave MY room to some administrator?"

"'Twas ever thus, Child. We have had the March of the

Ghastly Encroaching Offices for decades: more princi*pals*, fewer principles. This whole place used to be run from one little office suite. Now there are offices all over the joint—on every floor, in every wing. I've lost friends! One day, a classroom next door; the next, an office, a secretary, an administrator, and four thousand discipline cards."

"And so, all those people out there know about my room?"

"Yeah. They'd help you if they could. I would, too. But you're probably doomed to roam the earth with that damned grocery cart—like The Ancient Mariner—forever!"

And then, to cheer her up, he had told her more of the facts of life. "A parking lot conference can be social, racial, financial, pedagogical—or just gossip, in-house or district-wide. I learned a lot of the vital lessons out there: Try not to let them give you a class last hour of the day; never attempt to have a discussion during Period I; learn to eat fast; pee anytime you can get to a bathroom—target of opportunity and that sort of thing; never sit down without looking behind you at the chair—gum, you know; never turn your back on a class; befriend the secretary and the janitor; never never let the little bastards see you sweat."

"What is that teacher doing draped over the hood of that car?"

"Grading papers, Child. You grade papers anywhere you can, and anytime: toidy, in class, at meals, in traffic, in bed making love, before the TV or on the phone, during meetings, in the bath, on the exercise bike, in the dark . . ."

"In the dark?"

"Sure. Have a movie in class. Grade papers! Play a video tape. Grade papers. I even grade papers when I'm grading papers!"

"But, what if the kids try to cheat when you're grading papers?'

"Oh, they'll cheat! It's their right! Cheating is Freedom of Expression. Eighty-five percent of the honor students—in a recent poll, of course—admitted to cheating! They said the stress is too great; too much pressure to get high grades. So they cheat. The newspapers think we should make it easier for them so they don't have to cheat. The cheating is OUR fault! WE make them cheat! Since infancy, they haven't had to compete academically—so now, when they have to face the SAT, they're stressed. We're such monsters."

"What if we *catch* them cheating?"

"Just don't stress them about it! Poor things. And don't call their parents. They'll just tell you that everybody cheats—and ask you if you read the newspapers."

"Ah, the president."

"Besides, the kids have enough to worry about: whether to get their ears, nose, lip, navel, nipples or worse pierced; whether to live or die or have a manicure; whether to kill all of their friends or get a new backpack; whether to leave home to get away from a step-father who's raping them, or try to graduate. It's all here among our 2400."

"You are somewhat cynical."

"You think? I love these kids! There are just too many of them, and they're unsorted. But you will like teaching; it will get you to Heaven."

He mentored her. He warned her. He gave her coping skills. He even admitted that he loved those kids. She lasted a semester and a half. She had become an E-Worker and was safe now. She could have stuck around long enough to be snowed under by papers rather than real snow. She should shut up and leave Mr. Sherman alone. Nobody else on the faculty had a grocery cart, so shut up.

Well, he had *too* mentored her! He had made it clear that all teachers, like all beer truck drivers, know in their hearts that they do good! Detractors were out there, but so were zealots, fans, believers. He had advised her about teaching English. She had been taught that a collage was as good as an essay (no pesky grammar or punctuation to complicate matters). He just mentioned how bulky 180 collages would be, grocery cart or no—all that paste and glue, and perhaps corn and seeds, rope, hair, other objects. Glitter. A mess, really.

Well! When she had asked how to talk to a kid's probation officer, he had said, "Same method used in talking to a kid's pusher, pimp, parent, or lawyer: with witnesses!" Good advice. A smart teacher never talked to anyone alone. He had seen it all, so why not "share"? "Use your size, too. There is no masculinity in beating a tiny woman."

Everyone should have such a mentor. Mr. Sherman himself could have used such a mentor!—maybe even a grocery cart. God knows he always had a load of books and papers. Never a collage or diorama, but yearbook stuff for 17 years!

In his day, if you were writing, you wrote. That you could grade. How in the hell do you grade a collage?

The closest thing to a mentor that Mr. Sherman had ever encountered was a guy at the hospital when he was grading papers in the waiting room while his mother was dying. In the waiting room, lap full of papers, he was noticed by another worried man who was weary with pacing up and down and bug-eyed with coffee overdose.

"What's with the papers?"

"I'm an English teacher."

"English was my worst subject."

"I know."

"You know?"

"Yeah. It's always everyone's worst subject. It's the law."

"Lots of papers."

"Always. Tons of papers—real nightmare."

"Why do you assign so many?"

"Kids need to write a lot to learn to write."

"But if you don't wanna grade so many, order less!"

"I know. I could have collages. Or dioramas. But I can't grade collages or dioramas, so I make them write essays."

"Make them write less. Save yourself. Your eyes look like cranberries. Here you are at the hospital and your mother's in there close to death. You don't need that."

"Thank you. I'll take that under advisement."

The guy turned out to be a plumber, and he didn't have any pipes with him.

There had been an In-Service about it, as one might suspect. Ol' Shirley Knott herself presided, and the semi-formal, catered affair had taken place in the central administration building. It seemed so long ago.

"Hello, Old English Teachers! Today we are going on a really incredible journey into the world of 'Whole Language.' Can you say 'Whole Language'?"

"Hell no," replied the old English teachers—which sounded enough like Hello to get past Shirley Knott.

"Now, you old English teachers have been using red pens and pencils to 'correct' writing! That is now considered 'naughty'! It makes the hordes of young angels who wrote the papers feel bad. We even have heard of someone, we won't mention any names, who corrects spelling, grammar, paragraphing—and anything he can find! Can you say, 'naughty'?"

She then laid out the *whole language* approach to teaching English. The idea was to "empower" the student by accepting as gold any illiterate, fractured, run-on-ridden misspelled drivel a kid could crank out, without regard to paragraphing, sentence structure, continuity, or punctuation—so that the delicate child would "feel" good about his writing. He would receive no advice or criticism, no help or challenge. He would step out into the world confident, even arrogant, just bursting with self-esteem. And illiterate.

"And so we will practice together, Old English Teachers." Some papers were distributed, and the "grading" began. "First, everyone write—in black ink only—'Very Good!' Anywhere on the paper—it doesn't matter. Just write it. Then, somewhere else, write 'Thank you for sharing this with me.' And somewhere, write 'Perfect.' If you really have to slash and tear at their little egos, encircle a misspelled word and write, 'Oooops!' with a smiley face."

Of course, someone had a question: "Uh . . . Doctor Knott, do we actually read the paper?"

"Not necessarily, sir. That just shows your age. No, just write a lot of positive remarks and put a number on the paper."

A number. That took some probing, but the number was fully explained. A *five* would mean the child did not have a pulse, and no paper would ever get a *five*. A *four* would mean that he used both vowels and consonants. A *three* meant he had mastered the noun/verb nature of our language. A *two* was for noun/verb, plus left-to-right. A *one*? Well, if the paper appeared to make some kind of sense, it was top notch!

Mr. Sherman resolved to make rubber stamps with all the positive remarks, and probably the smiley face, too. Then he could rip through a stack of papers in a few minutes and go home to his wife. No problem.

Shirley Knott's parting words were, "These kids have torn these pages out of their very souls, Old English Teachers! We must honor that. Empower them. Empower yourself by giving your kids success."

"If we don't correct them, who will?" he wondered.

So he went away from the love-in quite empty, and, to the very last, he slashed and tore those papers, cut them to ribbons with a red pen. When he found mistakes, he marked them or fixed them. Thirty-seven years of kids had felt the sting of his red pen.

What a monster he had been.

Someone could have come up with *Cliffs Notes* on the piles of research papers—or maybe *Reader's Digest* could have done condensations. But, enslaved to the old ways, Mr. Sherman was condemned to reading those papers, even the ones with no articles or auxiliary verbs. He could not simply write, "Perfect" and let the thing go. The answer would have been half as many papers—half as many students. Too late for that now. He had done it the hard way, and there was no fixing that.

These days, Mr. Sherman found himself trying to read the newspaper without marking it up with a red pen. One local paper had a propensity for crediting ladies with 450 years of cooking experience, or announcing events for the 38th of July, or mourning the loss of someone who had been a local barber since 1748. A number thing. Another printed headlines like "Youth Charged With Battery." But the truth was, he did not read much at all—at the doctor's office maybe, or sometimes on a wild browse in a bookstore back in the city. But even that was work. The joy was gone. If Mr. Sherman had a tragedy in his life, this was it.

A pile of juicy books by Crichton or Grisham or King—along with Steinbeck and Hemingway, of course—and Minnesota boys like Lewis and Fitzgerald and Keillor—should have been by his bedside or handy somewhere out here in the living room so that he could fall into some other existence while up in the night lamenting things and going crazy. There should be a good book in any direction he extended his hand. That was part of the master plan. Everything he had missed, books he wanted to read again now that he was an old fogey, frivolous books never included in his education, books there had been no time for while mounds of ungraded papers rotted nearby, and winter books he had never read because there was no winter. He had owned all those books, but he had donated them to the school rather than move them up the mountain. Someday he would replace them in one fantastic visit to a half-priced book shop in the city. A lifetime of books.

He would get to them somehow, as soon as a desire for it returned—before weakening eyes or stomach problems or headaches destroyed the physical ability to sit and read, or lie and read, or stand or walk or lean or dangle, and read. Someday, or some night, he would love reading again. He would fix that, too! It would be part of sanity, of healing. To know about such wonders and not go there was inhuman.

What a trauma it had been, giving up the books. "I see cranberry," he could hear the delicate little interior decorator lisp. "I see kiwi, I see mango, I see puce." It was the day the biggest bookcase went. "Lose the books, lose the model ship, lose the globe. I see pampas grass . . ." The guy's wrists flapped in the breeze of the laboring air conditioner. The books had become furniture. The guy was right about that. And off they went to Hugh Stone High and oblivion, and the den was tricked out in cranberry, kiwi, mango, and puce.

Mr. Sherman flinched violently as the Regulator clock with the screwed-up hands struck 4:17. He was standing too close to it, looking again at his reflection in the black window. Predominantly dark hair with the hat off and no light behind it, inadequate fusilage hung with colorful fleece, utterly tasteless serape, English teacher glasses, and one cold hand with Diet Coke. Dork. Sixty. Alive.

"If you dress up, boys and girls, they will love reading. Wrap up in a sheet and read *Julius Ceasar*, become a puppet of Miss Piggy and read the role of Juliet; dress up like a grape and read Steinbeck."

Can you say "Bitch"?

Dressing up to sell the joy of reading probably would work. He thought of his "uniform" in his final year or two at the school: black slacks and polo shirt, school colors when possible. and he thought he heard derisive laughter among the kids. He had looked nerdy, dorky, more than likely. A 'geeze,' and intolerable.

The day he typed it up was memorable. He had been putting off the actual resignation letter, but one day it was obviously time to go.

Drinking fountains existed in the main hallways of Hugh Stone High, and there was water to be had early in the day. Later on, a disgusting stew of gum and spit and tobacco juice with stringy cuds developed, and drinking there became impossible. So the conversation that Mr. Sherman got in on that fateful day had probably taken place quite early.

A pierced, tattooed male, probably a Sophomore, swept back his ponytail, tipped his head to one side, and tried to take in some water, under the ring in his nose, over the silver knob in his tongue. He lifted up, and talked. "I mean, like, you know—I mean, cool, Dude."

Another identical creature replied, "&¢%$#%$#, Man—I went 'Hello,' and like she $%&¢%$in' went, 'Hey.' And then I was all &¢%$#&, Man, and she went %¢&¢%$#!"

The wet one responded, "Right! It was, Hey—you know?"

"Dude."

And they went off to class, having had a perfectly satisfying conversation. Mr. Sherman went home that afternoon and typed up his resignation—on a typewriter! Obviously, life as he knew it was over. Language was over. All progress since the cave man was over. Grunting and pointing was back. Getting out of there was sane. The resignation worked just fine.

Mr. Sherman looked at the Regulator clock again, trying to anticipate the next deafening jangle. He had tried to fix the thing, but the clock had a mind of its own. At seventeen minutes after the hour, or twenty-three, on Wednesday, but not Friday: glang glang glang; at thirteen minutes before the hour, maybe—or nine, but never anything divisible by five; and always always unanticipated. If you looked at it and waited, it would not chime at all. That would be too simple. He stared at it now, and waited.

A scream pierced the night, and Mr. Sherman was on the move again. He got everybody up out of their seats and tried to secure the room. The disaster drill was unscheduled, and so most classes were having final exams. They were going to be tough exams for the kids, because during the review week English teachers had taken the kids to the gym to look at the AIDS quilt, and then they took the TICT (Total Idiot's Communications Test). Now, during the actual final exam, they were running.

The Fire Marshal, when he was found, had footprints all over his body. He had decided to fling a *surprise* disaster drill, and he had positioned himself outside a classroom door in the Freshman wing. It was like standing by a Claymore mine at detonation. He was flung across the hall by the exploding door and trampled by the class from that side. He was not found for a while because in a disaster drill everyone is supposed to drop to the floor in the hallway and face the wall. The whole place looked like a mass grave, so he blended right in. Pity.

In Mr. Sherman's part of the building, the older kids were doing their thing: loud screaming, laughter, shadow-boxing, wrestling, feined humping doggy-style—the usual. Probably a good deal of information exchange, too—with all those final exams going on. Finally, they knelt down, heads covered, with teachers threatening genocide: peace! A complete disaster. Why do you think they called it a disaster drill?

Those caught having lunch in the giant lunch room when one of these drills occured were supposed to just drop everything and head for cover. Right. However, a disaster drill during lunch would be redundant anyway; a tornado during lunch would be redundant. A disaster drill OR lunch was tantamount to a terrorist attack—any day. Nuff said.

Always, as he now remembered, such drills were inconvenient—and that took planning. The Think Tank had to be at the bottom of that; it was all timed for maximum TSF points. Even a called-in bomb threat caused less trouble; but then, bombers are not as evil as those who plan other school events.

He remembered a day when Ol' Minnie Mae had come up with one of her tests—probably about something heady like controlling one's drool or something. The kids were hard at work, after the usual formal sit-down, listen-up, and don't write-until-I-tell-you-to routine. And the door to the classroom opened and two spacemen with a stepladder walked in. One-by-one, the kids lifted their heads from the intense work.

At last, everyone was of one mind. All seemed to say, "Okay. It figures. Do your worst."

This was the first wave of the "Asbestos Abatement" attack on Hugh Stone High. Someone had discovered asbestos in the building. Asbestos was against the newest rules, so it was abatement time. The men stood the ladder in the middle of the room somehow, encumbered by their EPA space suits, all silver and hooded and taped and hermetically sealed. Nobody else in the room, including Mr. Sherman who had lived there for two decades, had a space suit.

The men scraped a sample off the ceiling and carefully bagged it, being careful not to get any of it on them. They brought out peculiar instruments, and said, "Hmmmm."

"Hmmmm" was a word everybody knew about, so the kids decided to leave. Mr. Sherman, however, was able to stop them and get them back to work on the test.

The headlines, which he had now forgotten, probably said something like "Tests Show Kids Have Drool Control Problem" OR "Teachers Not Worth Spit" OR "Slobbering and Asbestos Not Related." Something nasty. Special drool funds would be sent, and new administrative offices would be built. Later, drooling would be deemed irrelevant.

But asbestos abatement became Mr. Sherman's favorite kind of abatement. Months and months of it, including a full summer, cleansed Hugh Stone High of asbestos. A simple broken window, however, was a spaceman call-up, because the old windows were mounted in asbestos putty or something wonderful.

"Hell, Boy, EPA was a Godsend. We wuz out of disruptions! Asbestos abatement: a whole new world!"

"I'll drink to that," muttered Mr. Sherman. With Coke, he drank to that wonderful era. And now a dry cup. Time to shuffle into the kitchen for a re-fill. He was using a little plastic glass stolen from a motel, to keep down the intake. Nothing complicated about that little cup. Except that it winked at him.

Damned if the cup didn't wink! Winked at him like it knew something terribly confidential.

"Then comes my fit again!" he moaned. That wink!

There is a type of fame involved with being a teacher. After a few years, the world has a sprinkling of people who recognize you and want to walk up to you in Guam or some other exotic place and say, "Mr. Sherman! Gee, you were my favorite English teacher. English was my worst subject. You haven't changed a bit. Are you still at Hugh Stone High?"

Mr. Sherman had encountered his kids in other cities, in other states, on other continents, at the bank, at the grocery—even at a strip joint he was dragged to between marriages (totally against his will, kicking and screaming all the way, of course).

But the wild days between marriages were over. All the moonlight gambling, the risky behavior, the seemingly endless wandering, the irregular hours—over! And grading papers in all those odd places was over, too. A new wife, a new life, stability, and rescue—renewal was the reality now. And so was the trip to the friendly neighborhood vasectomy clinic.

Under any circumstances, it would have been difficult to go there, turn himself in, and have himself whacked. He had reviewed all the material, he had seen the pictures and diagrams, he had screamed, and he had decided. As he entered the chop shop (totally against his will, kicking and screaming all the way), only one thing really bothered him: Why would he be unable to drive afterward? If it was such a "simple office procedure," why would driving be so difficult? Legitimate concern.

Whereas Mr. Sherman had never been in combat or taught in junior high, he was a gutsy guy; so he could do this thing. The valiant only taste of death but once.

But there was a girl at the clinic: little Leticia Sanchez, two years out of Hugh Stone High. And she was wearing white!

"Mr. Sherman! Gee, I can't believe it's you. You were my favorite English teacher. English was my worst subject. You haven't changed a bit. Are you still at Hugh Stone High?" And, finally, "How may I whack you?"

Well, maybe she said "help," but whack was on his mind, and whack was what he heard.

Mr. Sherman was disarmed. "I am here to be disarmed," he said. "It's a birthday present for my wife—the lady over there with the 357 magnum."

"No problem," said the girl, "It's a simple office procedure." The women made eye contact with each other.

Victory.

"So nice to see you again, Letty. Will you be in the room?"

"In the room?" she asked with feined innocence.

"Yeah. In the room. For the..uh . . . procedure."

"Oh, no. I'm not a nurse yet. I guess you're just lucky." Letty managed a little giggle. Mr. Sherman girded his loins.

The whacking went well, as whackings go. Wifey drove him home. He was simply not aggressive enough for city traffic anymore. That was what it was all about. He had left his manhood back there in that office. He would probably not get on the freeway for weeks. But the whacking itself was a walk in the park, really. No biggy. He graded four themes while it was going on. Piece of cake.

It is after the procedure that things get weird. There comes a day when you have to go back to the clinic and prove that the procedure worked—that persistent little squigglers haven't found an alternative route. A specimen, then, has to get into a cup somehow, and that cup has to be handed to the girl in the office. And, as she receives that cup, the girl knows how the specimen got into the cup. She knows. No two ways about it.

Okay, a thousand cups, a thousand specimens, a thousand guys, right? But her English teacher? Mister? The word is, "Aaarrrrggghhh!"

Don't be ridiculous. She can't even pretend she doesn't know!

"We have come a long way since English 4B, Letty," Mr. Sherman said wearily, handing her the cup with wan dignity.

"I know that's right," she said. And she winked. Damned if she didn't wink! And she received the cup.

After that, he wouldn't have needed a vasectomy at all—ever! All the fight had gone out of him. The upside? He was not called back to be re-whacked or anything. Success.

Life is unfair. It *was* nice seeing Letty again—seeing her at work doing her job, aspiring, orbiting off into the world of work. Winking. The alcohol smell of that clinic, the casual, routine, matter-of-fact gelding that happened there, and that damned cup were enough to keep a man up all night unassisted by other nightmares.

Mr. Sherman set the cup down and stared out the black window. Out there in the night he supposed there were just legions of teachers encountering their former kids in somewhat strained circumstances: like being prepped for surgery or bathed in a hospital bed, or trained on the computer in a classroom, or given a speeding ticket in traffic. It must happen as much as grocery store contacts or casual fellow-traveler encounters. Normally, a teacher would be embarrassed by his own ignorance, proud of the kid, glad the kid was okay.

Mr. Sherman's experience had just been more intense than that, that's all. Probably quite harmless, really. And yet, something deep inside said, "Aaarrrggggh!"

He had been able to muster enough testosterone to rejoin city traffic, but it always seemed, after the fateful whacking, that a man in a brown truck had taken up following him. Wherever he went in that traffic hell, there was the brown truck, with a man who looked different each time but was no doubt the same guy: brown outfit, shorts in summer. And the truck: no door on the driver's side, back part a closed box, brown and mysterious. Probably something the Think Tank set upon him: some fellow whackee, a member of a cult of brown geldings out recruiting.

Maybe not. But the Think Tank was always working on something. No denying it: those trucks were everywhere, even in these hills.

"There! Did y'all see that, Doctor Harm?"

"I think so, Dr. Billy Joe et cetera. I think so . . ."

"Y'all sound so tentative. No question about it, far's ah'm concerned. There was a blip. Dr. Minnie Mae Honey, y'all in charge of testin'—what's yer take on this?"

They were all wearing lab coats, and a kid was hooked up

to a bunch of wires. Mr. Sherman knew this was going to be good. Triggered by the lab coats, most likely.

"It's perfectly clear to me," said Dr. Minnie Mae. "In the remotest corner of this Senior's cerebellum, there is a small but definite cluster of cells exhibiting intermittent electrical activity!"

"And that's official?"

"My final answer."

"Son, what we're lookin' at here is another college-bound kid, the product of all our efforts these many years. Some of 'em tried to shut the doors and teach him somethin'; they tried keepin' him in Middle School—but he got too old; they gave him F's finally D minuses to keep him out of college. They hit him with programs, classifications, vocational counseling. The S.A.T. had a shot at him. But off to college he goes."

"The professors will love that! They'll write books complaining about dumb kids getting to college. This is a fun job, Dr. Boss."

"Kid'll be outa there by Christmas, but they'll git his money fer awhile. Wake him up, Dr. Minnie Mae, and show him how the doorknob works."

"You know," said Dr. Harm, "I have an idea—a really strange idea."

"Gather round, girls; Ol' Dr. Son here has his lab coat on and he's got an idea. Life is good. Son, the floor is yours."

Dr. Harmon Bullington's excitement here would be almost uncontrollable. "All right! Look: we are going to blame these kids' last teachers for the whole 13 years of dumbing down and neglect and all that, right?"

"Well, sure, Son, but . . ."

"I say we tattoo 'em!"

"What?"

"Tattoos! We make the teachers actually sign their

work! A kid can't add? His math teacher signs him!"

"Right on the butt! Ah luv it, Dr. Harm! By-God genius!"

"A kid can't read and write? His Senior English teacher signs him! He can't identify Thomas Jefferson? Adam Smith? Richard Nixon? His last history teacher . . ."

"Signs his butt! Make 'em own up to bein' the author of all that kid's ignorance! It's a great idea. We'll get it goin' by 2002, fer sure!" Dr. Billy Joe et cetera would hawk up a great black cud and propel it into the void. "Pass the buttermilk," he would say. "I'm workin' here."

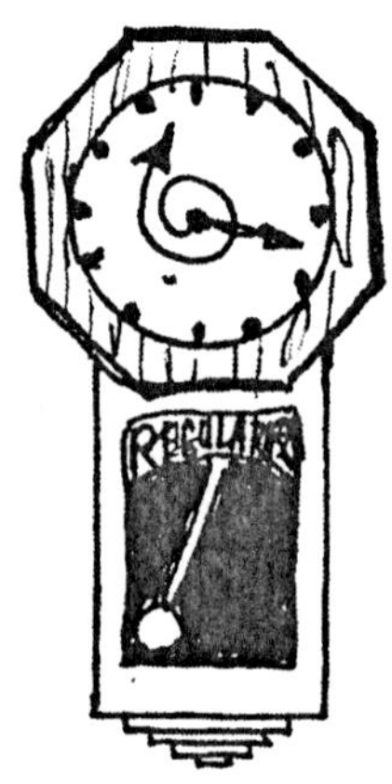

Chapter Twelve

It was good to be alone with this thing. A mild shudder went through him as he stepped over to the sliding glass door for another investigation of the storm, the storm he had come to see and hear and feel. Things were smoothing out. Mistakes made in setting the house and garage, in cutting the driveway, in marrying the work of man to the work of mountain, were being put aright by the wind and snow. And, more than likely, a hell of a lot of work was being created out there, too.

Not long ago, the electricity would have been knocked out by a storm like this, Mr. Sherman had been told by his new neighbors. But things had gone underground. The winds could howl, and the ice could build up, but the power would flow. And if something did cut off the electricity, the all-important telephones would still operate. He had seen the fiber optics cable threaded into a slot in the ground right under where Miss Whitby was standing with her stolen grocery cart. Under her frozen feet: messages flowing back and forth in a miraculous system few really understood.

"Hello, Dr. Billy Joe et cetera? 'Sears Ol' Ernie Carson

up in Washington."

"Damn, Boy, y'all caught me at a good tahm! Ol' Minnie Mae and me's just finishin' up a meal: ate our first-bornt child jist now! Had 'im on ahss! Then we micro-waved the cat, and we tossed a mess o' puppies onto the freeway. We feelin' good. What's up with y'all?"

"Ah got a bunch o' good news fer y'all Ejamakators down there—money news!"

"Y'all a man after mah own heart! My ol' daddy always said, 'Money is the root of all bad.' So, lemme have it, Boy!"

"Well, 'member all that Dumbin' Down business?"

"Shore do: one of our finest conspiracies."

"Well, that took some doin' and it took some money. So now that y'all got 'em dumbed way the hell down, we gonna send y'all twice as much to smarten 'em back up! The natives is restless."

"Figgers."

"So, y'all still got Ol' Minnie Mae humpin' away at the Dumbin' Down?"

"That's Doctor Minnie Mae, Son. And, yup—still got her pluggin' away."

"Well, y'all gotta promise that she'll be in charge of smartenin' 'em back up. Kin ah count on y'all?"

"Not jist yes, but Hell Yes! Only, why does it gotta be Ol' Dr. Minnie Mae?"

"Consistency."

There would be a long pause, then both men would howl with laughter for two minutes.

"Consistency! Son, that was funny!"

"Jist change a few words here an' there, reverse a few instructions, throw in a slogan or two."

"Sounds like a plan, Boy!"

"Now, we gonna send you a shitload o' money, and we're talkin' Programs, here, Dr. Billy Joe, Programs!"

Ol' Billy Joe et cetera's eyes would light up and become

significantly larger. "Gotcha! We gonna call it somethin' like . . ." And he would ponder a second or two, but, understand, Dr. Billy Joe et cetera did not have to lie awake at night to think this stuff up. He was on the case in an instant. "Somethin' like, 'Back to Brains,' or 'Private School Results in Public Schools,' or 'Knowledge BEFORE College'—gotta be somethin' simple, cuz folks cain't hardly read anymore."

"How y'all gonna communicate with these fools if they runnin' around mystified by alphabet soup?"

"The teachers, Boy! The teachers! Jist tell 'em we gonna pull another 180, and turn 'em loose. They used to it by now, them that's still around."

"Now, now we cain't go to givin' all this money to a bunch o' pissant teachers . . . !"

"Oh, Hell no! We give it to the PROGRAM! That means more offices, secretaries, files, computers, sub-assistant vice principals. Jist send me about a boxcar full o' crystal apples, Son. They got 'em by the dozens when we wuz dumbin' down, and they'll work jist as hard with the smartenin' up!"

"No way they'll go fer that again!"

"They have to, Boy! They gonna be the ones on the spot! Accountability, Son—accountability! 'Sides, the future o' their country depends on it!" And he would place his hand over the spot where, on most people, there would be a heart. "Y'all jist send us the bucks, and ah'll git out mah ol' sermons, and we'll git everybody convinced that this is brand new, the latest thing, and By-God indispensible. Jist hide and watch."

Maybe Ol' Billy Joe would have a small American flag in the mix somewhere, as red smoke rose around him.

"Got the Fourth Estate all set up," Carson would brag. "They gonna say, 'These inept teachers got us into this mess, and it's time to clean house. They cain't make up their minds what they're doin'—no wonder the kids is the worst students in the known world.' And then there oughta be another round of scholarly books and articles that'll absolutely . . ."

"Piss everybody off!"

"*Big* Time! By God, life is good, ain't it, Billy Joe?"

"That's Doctor Billy Joe, Son—let's not forget about our dignity!" And the two of them would howl.

"Oh, say, we jist wanted t' ask y'all, too: y'all got this computer all figured out yet?"

"Use it all the tahm . . ."

"Well, it should be in every phase of the operation by now: yer schedulin', yer grades, yer payroll, yer logistics—everthin'."

"We're with yuh, Son. What's yer point?"

"Well, it's been found that y'all kin take them grades an' cut some throats with 'em. What percentage o' the kids fail a certain teacher's course? Was that fair? What percentage of what sex or race get A's? We got us a Mexican lesbian on the loose? What percentage of what sex or what religion or ethnicity git the conduct cuts? You with me, Dr. Billy Joe?"

"Oh, we on it, all right—we on it like ticks on a long-haired dog. We nailed one ol' boy fer too many failures in class o' 18-year-old Freshmen—all of 'em wuz criminals, minority, and A.D.D., too: very sensitive area."

"Hope y'all fahrd that ol' boy."

"Nope. Took his retirement and went away. We runnin' so low on teachers we jist decided to pull folks in off the street to set in the rooms!"

(That's how they got Deeton out. Some said it was because a kid called him 'Dude,' but Mr. Sherman knew the truth.)

"Good part is, y'all kin jist blame it all on the computer. Computer says this; computer says that. It's the modern age! And stick it all into their records, all this crap—use it against 'em in the next assessment! 'Computer says you a racist, Boy!' God, Ah luv it!"

"Life is good."

"Oh, one more thang: we got money all over the place comin' down there fer Vouchers—send kids to private schools? Well, we gonna get 'em hooked, and then we gonna jerk that rug out from under 'em—drop 'em right on their noses—whip them li'l peckerwoods back into public schools, real sudden, with the savages again!"

"That oughta clear some sinuses! Damn, Boy, y'all gittin' jist diabolical!" And they would cackle about that word.

"Guess we're whut's called a *loose cabal*!"

Sardonic laughter then, squirting through the fiber optics cable under Miss Whitby's feet out in the frozen driveway. Yeah, it would still be going on like that, with or without Mr. Sherman, until the process itself burnt out.

Okay, there had to be a reason greater than making everybody mad. Usually, these things are about money. Maybe the country was creating a population totally dependent upon machines to hold and develop knowledge—just to sell the machines. Maybe somebody up there was trying to bring it all down by dumbing it all down. Someday, someone would flip a switch somewhere and the population wouldn't know its butt from third base—and wouldn't even know how to look it up! If an alien entity landed and stated its intention to do such a thing to us, there would be a war—and Mr. Sherman would come out of retirement for it! Kick some alien butt.

Such rhetoric, Mr. Sherman!

He had seen a movie about a millionaire industrialist who bought grades and diplomas for his kid all the way through college, and then was stuck with a babbling numbskull that he wanted to be his company's C.E.O. Talk about remediation! That looked familiar to Mr. Sherman. Could this mess have happened because of well-meaning fools?

Naw. Mr. Sherman decided that it was just Evil again: a simple case of Teachers vs. Evil, mankind hanging in the balance. Same old same old.

Evil. Evil visited Mr. Sherman regularly. He was a veteran of that fight. It came in many forms.

Form #X711513 was in his mail box after school one Wednesday in what would have been Spring in most parts of North America. It was never good to receive an X711513, but here it was, on Hump Day, smoldering and reeking. It was tentamount to a summons: a parent conference was afoot.

It would happen Thursday.

"Aaaarrrggghhh!"

Mr. Sherman did the drill: whipped out the grade book, looked up the kid's recent grades, called up all recent memories of contact with the kid, popped two antacid tablets and three aspirins, and found a paper scheduled to be returned to the kid. This was going to be thorny.

This was going to be a meeting that called forth all of the self-discipline and basic decency he could muster. He was through with Old Hugh Stone High, just tying up a few loose ends. It was particularly bad to cross Mr. Sherman at this time for any reason. He would owe nobody anything at that meeting, not even the Vice Principal, his friend. He would have a chip on his shoulder. "Make my day, Suckuh!" If some raving lunatic parent came flying across a table at him with her sharp white teeth and her cranberry eyes, he would club her down like a dog. That would be disappointing and unprofessional. He could almost hear her neck snapping.

"I demand a Margarita meeting. Today."

"Granted. But on Wednesday, Mr. Sherman? You shock me," Jerry said, stroking his beard.

"I have great need."

"Parent conference, huh?"

"Yeah. Vice Principal, parent, kid, me, counselor, and of course, security."

"Meet you in the cave in twenty minutes."

It turned out that Wednesday was an excellent day for a

Margarita meeting. Very therapeutic. The whole gang made it by five. It was a recognized emergency. It was clear that Mr. Sherman needed to be slowed down, soothed, pacified, prepared, assured. This was done.

And after the Wednesday meeting, he went to the Thursday Parent Conference . . . well, what's the word? Empowered. He was By-god Empowered! When he walked into the little room, his mob went in with him, in spirit. So, this was team building! He could feel his friends at his elbow, nudging him, whispering in his ear.

The kid looked quiet enough, and so did the mother. But they can turn on you. It's a house of cards. These are wild creatures, thought Mr. Sherman: I must not make any threatening moves.

He sat down and made sure his head was lower than any other head in the room.

"Mr. Sherman, this young lady is worried about her English grade—particularly her recent theme grade." The vice Principal looked weary and businesslike; but, empowered now, Mr. Sherman felt sharp and fresh.

He whipped out the old grade book, but of course he knew his ground and the girl's grades. "The theme was written in class and it earned a C," he stated firmly.

"That's tellin' her," Colleen whispered.

"I don't get it," said the mother, a sane enough looking lady in her late thirties. "We always get an A or a B on our themes."

"Hear that . . . ? SHE writes the damn papers," hissed Darby.

"Yes, on papers written at home—or simply downloaded at home," Mr. Sherman offered politely. "But this one was done in the classroom, with no Spell-Check, No Internet, No Mommy, No Ghost Writer of any kind. This is what the kid can do."

"Well, why do you even do such things? My daughter can't get grades like this! She was all alone in there with nothing but a pen and some paper—not even her own paper, but paper you provided!"

Mr. Sherman smiled.

"And you expected her to write about something you discussed behind my back in class! What's up with that?"

"*Careful now,* " *intoned Jerry.*"

"*Tell her to go to Hell!*" *coached Darby.*

"Just like the good old days," he said—but nice. Mr. Sherman was nice. Composed.

"But, Mr. Sherman, you expected this girl to write this paper with no mechanical help? No crutch of any kind? Just like that?" The Vice Principal was getting it.

"I didn't even let her buy a vowel."

"*Atta Boy,*" *said the mob.*

"Hear that? He can't do that! She gets to use a calculator in math class, and all he lets her have is a pen?"

"*Leave my math class out of this, Bitch!*" *rasped Darby.*

"There are dictionaries in the room. Books!" said Mr. Sherman very calmly.

"But alone? Where was her team? Her Group? You didn't even let them talk to each other."

"What can I say? Life is unfair. She was on her own in there. She earned a C." Still dignity. Composure. Calm.

"I don't like your attitude, Mister!" The lady bristled now.

"I feel your pain," he remembered from somewhere.

"*Almost Presidential,*" *he heard Colleen giggle.*

"But a C. What are you trying to do to my little girl?"

"Glad you asked. First, the basic skills: reading, writing, grammar. Then, the knowledge: information, facts—from English literature. Then, a system or method of putting it together: an essay in this case. Practice. This was practice. Life comes later. Three weeks hence, I believe."

"*Very good. Almost a philosophy of Education!*" *said Jerry.*

"But what's wrong with the computer?"

"It's one of the tools, but it is not her brain—not yet! She had to be more than a girl with a mouse and a mommy this time." But he meant that in the best possible way.

He expected her to come flying across the table any second now, but she sat tight.

"But, Mr. Sherman, a *C*?"

"She earned it. All by herself."

The lady rose with dignity, and so did Mr. Sherman.

"Twenty years ago," she said, "you gave *me* A's!"

"Those were the good old days," he said, not even blinking. After he faced the girl at the vasectomy clinic, this was nothing. He began to recognize the lady.

"But I still don't like your attitude."

"What can I say? Life's a bitch!"

"No! You did not say that! Tell me you did not say that." Colleen would have been so disappointed if it were true.

"Well, maybe I didn't use that exact phraseology. But, my God, this gal was surreal. Evidently, I should just say to the kids, 'Everybody go home and pull up a good theme about young John Keats, print it out, and hand it in! Or have your mom handle it: as I remember, she was pretty good!"

"But the bottom line is, you got through the parent conference, Mr. Sherman," said Jerry. "That calls for a celebration."

"I'll drink to that. Any new business?"

"Wait a minute! I feel unfulfilled here. What happened with the kid and her paper?" asked Darby.

"Kid got a C on her paper. Nuff said." Hefty, salty sip right about there.

"But that's what she had going in!"

"Life's a bitch, and now you can quote me."

And Friday's meeting raged on.

It was all about healing after the indignities of the week. Oh, he had considered letting the lady have it, for all of the teachers in all of the parent conferences in all of the world—just touch off a broadside and pound her to mush—for all of the misguided thinking of all of them. But the lady was not her own fault. She was the result of a fully-funded, deliberate program—an outrage gone mad: a system that took care of body and soul and left the mind blank—that cranked out perfectly self-confident, well-adjusted kids who were semi-literate. And he had been part of the system, by default.

Looking back on it now, he realized that he had been trained to feel responsible for and take the heat for that failed system, that thrown fight. And that, too, was part of the system.

Chapter Thirteen

The whole house seemed darker now as the thickening storm gripped Mr. Sherman's mountain. Powdery clouds of snow swathed the yard light, stopped up all access to outside light, obcured the windows. How he loved it.

The recliner was occupied, and the 'doctor' was in.

"You're back," he informed the spectre.

"Thou art not yet healed. I am returnéd."

"You could have saved yourself the trip. I'm fine."

"Thy shame must be faced and vanquished."

"Look, I already admitted to the *Cliffs Notes* thing. And the hug business was . . . was . . ."

"Nothing. Nay, thy shame lies deeper, Mister!" And there was a definite mocking tone to that "Mister."

"I have accepted that I was guilty of doing my lesson plans after . . ."

"Bigger!"

"Bigger?"

"Aye. Thy shame lies deeper, longer—career-long."

The Shrink looked strange now—enigmatic—a little too creepy, like he was *acting*—rather badly.

"But I was right about retiring! I know that now: It was no mistake; I was burnt out; it was only fair to the kids that I quit."

"Thy shame lies not in that vain thought. Others will teach. 'Tis thou must learn from thyself!"

"Riddles! I'm cracking up here, and you sit over there in the shadows and spout riddles. I don't need this!"

"Well put," the spectre said. Then all the Shakespeare, Stratfordian and Oxfordian, went out of him; he softened, looked a lot like Jerry for a moment, tossed in a dash of Ol' Billy Joe et cetera, and finished with a goodly strain of Sherm himself! He now reminded Mr. Sherman of the guy down at the feed store in the village.

"This could have been fun," said the Shrink. "We could have really had a conversation here, leading to a new level of self-awareness on your part. But no: you had to get impatient!" The character began tapping his fingers on the arm of the chair.

"I don't need fun here. I need to get a grip—by sun-up!"

"Okay, Dipstick. Hit the couch and think with me. Now!"

The gloves were off now. This was going to be real. Mr. Sherman hit the couch.

"Let her rip, Freud—she'll tear anyway!" Too long in the hills.

"Do you believe that you sold out?"

"Sure. Daily. Often. On a regular basis. I sold out all the time."

"You tried the methods they advocated?"

"Yes. That was the sell-out."

"Did you pamper the students?"

"Sometimes. Too often. It was fashionable, so I pampered."

"Did you buy into a phenomenon called 'Cooperative Learning'?"

What a terrible thing to bring up! This was a nightmare

so twisted that Mr. Sherman had always passed credit for it way up the line to the Think Tank itself.

"I couldn't do that stuff! Yeah, I tried it, but you can't have a committee write things. Collective thinking is a fraud. You can't put kids in a group and expect anything but chaos. Someone always hides out. I hid out myself when we ran models. It was just a fancy way for teachers to abdicate their responsibilities. I faked it when I did it."

"What about Direct Teaching?"

"Big new thing, huh? Sure, they brought that back like it was something new, but *that* was me all along!"

"Did you correct kids?"

"Yes."

"Did you make them memorize things?'

"Yes."

"Did you give objective tests? Require kids to know facts?

"I did. I did all that."

"And you made them drill, didn't you? And you marked up their spelling and subject/verb agreement!'

"Yes, yes!" Mr. Sherman's tortured voice no longer sounded like his own. "*They* called it busywork!"

"You hated the Whole Language approach, didn't you! You pushed phonics and standard English all those years! You even had those kids identifying nominative absolutes and retained objects!"

"Yes, God help me, I did!"

"You set up competitive situations in your classes—you spotlighted superior work and good students!" The Shrink was coming on like a prosecuting attorney.

"I admit it. I had vocabulary tests and spelling tests—objective! And regularly! For Seniors! They didn't have any tools!"

"And you graded the papers."

"I did. I gave A's, but I gave F's, too. I let kids fail if that was what they wanted to do."

"You certainly did. You were never considered a modern teacher—not by your superiors! For shame!"

"It's true . . . true. A modern teacher would not allow failure. Today's kids have success all the way to illiteracy."

"You set deadlines, marked mistakes on papers . . . '

"They had to know what they were doing wrong!"

"You taught fundamentals, you maverick! You yelled at those kids, teased them, used sarcasm, chided, pushed, cajoled."

"They didn't get cajoled anywhere else! That was a ten dollar word. Look, I was playing catch-up ball! They were so far behind when we got them!" Mr. Sherman's eyes began getting rather wet. Go figure.

"You joked with them, made them laugh at you, entertained them! If there was no class clown, YOU were the class clown!"

"Such a ham."

"You made them write poetry—with rhyme and meter!"

"What can I say? Free verse can be just drivel. They needed rules!"

"Indeed."

"I even made them document quotations! I was bad."

"You socialized, too—even to the point of touching them! Time was, you hugged! You loved those damned kids at one time. In fact, you did all the things The Bastards told you not to do!"

"And I only did what they wanted me to in my 'Dog and Pony' shows at assessment time . . . . Saved my rear."

"Complete rebellion! You simply were not part of the big educational endeavor of your time."

"I know . . . I know . . . . I made them sit in rows!"

"Mister Sherman, you even lectured!"

"Aaaarrrrggggghh! I know. I lectured the soup out of them. Rather well at times. And I made them take notes. I was so bad."

"And did you tell them about *Cliffs Notes*?"

"Yeah—and Monarch—and a hundred other short-cuts."

"Tools."

"Yes. But Dylan Thomas is tough, and T.S. Elliot—and we were out of time—always out of time! Damned tests and pictures and AIDS quilts and mundane bull . . ."

"You went to the beach with those kids."

"I went *pheasant hunting* with some of those kids! We wrote plays and skits, talked drama at pizza parties, did plays, put together yearbooks. I knew some of them as people!"

"Idiot! You could have been busted at any time. You were lucky. You placed yourself in their hands. You trusted those people."

"I did. I had to! God, when I think about it, I plotted and schemed with them—made deals—conned them—tricked them and kidded myself! I never told them what I was doing to them until it was done!"

"You fiend! No ELO's? In an Outcome-based Program? You *were* bad!"

"And, while we're at it, I blew off three of their most potent In-Service Sessions—the pride of Shirley Knott herself: one on 'Lock-Step Conformity,' one on 'Supervised Spontaneity,' and one on 'Large-Group Individuality.'"

"Also, you believed in Ability Grouping all along, didn't you?"

"Yes, I would have prayed for it right in school if it had not been so risky to do so. It's true. I could never see why some genius should have to wait—or why some slow kid should have to have that genius rubbed in his face every day."

"But what about Equity!"

"Screw Equity! It's not fair."

"What about Inclusion?"

"Screw Inclusion, too. Why should some psycho have a forum in my classroom with my normies and my dummies—and my Chinese scholars and my wonderful kids from Cameroon?"

"Fairness, Mr. Sherman, Fairness!"

"But not Carte Blanche!"

"You didn't even like that Utopian school with no bells, no walls, no windows, no strata, no categories, no competition, no grades . . ."

"No learning, no teaching . . . . No deal! No. I did not like it—I hated it—tried to clean up its mess before turning the kids it crippled loose into the world, to make up for lost time."

"But there should be time for childhood."

"Not 18 years."

"You did not participate in American Education in your time, then."

"I guess not. American Public Education was the least American thing we had going. Americans win."

The spectre/shrink began humming "America the Beautiful," rather mockingly.

"If a kid doesn't know anything, how can he choose, and cope, and connect!? The competition *knows!*"

"Exactly."

"All that sitting in circles, carrying your gray matter in an instrument holstered on your hip, playing patty-cakes, cutting and pasting and coloring—in high school!? I couldn't do it. I shut my door. They brought new teachers fresh out of college who knew MTV and Bill Gates."

"You were old-fashioned—outdated."

"Archaic! I was a relic of a time when schools got kids ready for life."

"A dinosaur.'

"Geeze—old bastard.'

"Narrow-minded, intolerant of run-on sentences, mall talk, Ebonics, vocal static, jibberish, spelling and punctuation errors . . ."

"Anything that would make the kid look stupid."

"You could literally have had the villagers come after you with pitchforks, do you realize that?"

"I expected it daily."

"And you freely admit it: you never wanted the parents in the building!"

"Not in the city! They lost their value system somewhere. The ones who could read got into books that told them how to interfere rather than participate. They twisted their kids and sent them to us and tried to jump in after them and blame us. Someone in our profession should have stood in the schoolhouse door and said, '*&¢%$#$ off! We will handle school: you go get a home going.'"

"You were bad, Mr. Sherman!"

"I know, I know. But I was right."

"If you were right, you were right to leave. You should sleep. In your room, you did what you could. Right?"

"Right. And I know it happened in a lot of rooms, with the door shut."

"And then you pooped out, and the money was right, and you retired. And it's snowing." Now, *that* was sanity!

Mr. Sherman smiled—got cold teeth right there in his living room. The Regulator clock chimed some ridiculous odd numbered minute—another thing we had been unable to fix. He didn't even look at the clock. The clock was right when it was wrong, and he was right when he left. Life is unfair.

Maybe a higher power had been in it with him all along. He had blown through it without the expected infamy—ruin—disgrace, maintaining a low profile. He had achieved the promised mountain. And now it was all making sense. He began feeling sane—sane and comfortable—warm and sleepy, and adjusted. He dismissed the imaginary shrink with a blink of the eye. He had reached a handy little accomodation with his futile career.

Outside, the snow swirled up in a blinding cloud. And so he projected himself into the white, cold cloud for one last fantasy, steering, in full control.

Mr. Sherman was finishing a nearly impossible climb up a windy, sleet-pelted stone cliff, his fingers ragged and bleeding, his knees and elbows and ankles scraped raw. But now, at the top, he at last approached his goal: a tall, stainless steel podium, simple, but official-looking, like a customs gate or that little rostrum for the maitre d' at a good restaurant." But the sign said, "Surrender."

A stainless steel man was standing there, swathed in an icy vapor, holding a stainless steel pen and a stainless steel phone clamped to his shoulder by his tilted head—or vice versa.

"I am here to surrender," said Mr. Sherman.

The stainless steel man raised a finger and pointed at him, but listened to the little phone and kept writing, tongue visible in the corner of his mouth.

"I am here—what's left of me," Mr. Sherman said. "I am through down there. I was a teacher, you know. I think we had a deal. I'm turning myself in." He was babbling.

The stainless steel man covered the phone for a moment and addressed Mr. Sherman with a knowing, kindly expression. "Get to you in a minute, Sir. Hold still."

"Hold still? Hmmmm. Strange." But he was in no condition to be impatient. Hold still. He had been a little hyperactive himself, now that he considered the prospect. "Okay. I can wait. No hurry. No problem. Don't mind me. As you were! I'll just hold still. Relax. I have time. Retired. No big deal. Smoke 'em if you've got 'em. Don't worry; be happy. Take your time. Sorry about this. Didn't mean to be a burden. Guess you're busy. No—really! Got all day! I'm fine. It's cool. Do what you have to do. I'm not here." He reached for some papers to grade—some old conditioned response, no doubt.

The stainless steel man finally finished the phone session. "Now, then!" he said loudly—to stanch the flow. "You are a 'Surrender'?"

"That is correct," said Mr. Sherman, lower lip aquiver.

"Had enough, huh? Well, your troubles are over, Sir. Just fill out this form, being careful not to bleed on the critical parts, and then check off all the things you could not do."

A stack of papers three feet tall was wheeled out on a stainless steel freight dolly.

"Is that . . . ?"

"That is the form and the list. Simply place a check mark beside each item you recognize as something you could not do: arts, sciences, crafts, miracles, levitations, transmutations, cures, surgical procedures . . ."

"The ones I could NOT do . . . ?"

"Should keep you busy. Oh, I believe you say 'Fix'—these are things you could not fix. Like the clock, the Ph.D. envy, the emasculation, etc."

"Oh."

"And when you are finished, Sir, you will go to Teacher Heaven, where there are no eight o'clock classes, no classes larger than twenty, no criminal lunatics in the room, and you get an hour for lunch."

"Will I get paid?"

"No more food stamps for you! The kids will pay attention, laugh at your jokes, and have plenty of self-esteem because they really know and can do things. And there will be a restroom next door. Sainthood is automatic."

"Coke machine?"

"Two doors down on the left."

"What about administrators?"

"There are no administrators in Teacher Heaven. Of course, if you insist, one can be brought up especially for you from Teacher Hell."

"Where is Teacher Hell?"

"Mr. Sherman, you will know this administrator on sight."

Mr. Sherman's mind clouded, then cleared abruptly. "Then where I was—that was Teacher Hell?"

"Absolutely."

He accepted a stainless steel pen and sat down to his last big batch of papers. The ink was red. In the hours that followed, Mr. Sherman found 1126 errors, mainly spelling. And he marked them all, and he felt warm.

Back at the black window, with a crooked little smile, he said, "Cuz that's the kind of guy (pause) I am!" He adjusted his little flat hat, trying for jaunty, trying for whimsical. He was going to make it now. No sweat.

Not only that, but something having to do with being sixty years old now shouted at him to stay inside, bundle up very warm, and forget all about any damned fool adventure hike into the snowy canyon out back. This was an urge he could understand. He resolved to write to Garrison Keillor and get a holy dispensation.

Chapter Fourteen

The Regulator clock with the screwed-up hands sang its morning song—a noise a lot like its mid-afternoon song and its middle-of-the-night screams: not noticeably more cheerful or pleasing and still random. Un-fixed. That clangor failed to harmonize with the hum of the yard light just outside as its sensor picked up on the first glows of morning—the first light to get through the clouds and the falling snow. The hum was winding up, accelerating, and soon the yard light would shut off. Gray and murky as it was, this was the light of the new day, and it was technically acknowledged by machine, making impending sunrise official.

The sound, not the light, roused Mr. Sherman. Damned annoying, that clock. He opened his eyes, assessed the light, and concluded for himself that he had made it through another night. He rose like some sort of salvaged vessel, shook off the clinging weeds of sleep, and tested his balance and buoyancy. He was "good to go."

He moved to the glass door and gazed out into the brightening gray and checked the snowy vista for fragments of the familiar: pieces of fence or wall, of tree or bush. A birdhouse with a comical tilted hat—not the closest item, but somehow the zaniest, the most 'country'—made him smile. Then a circle grabbed his eye: the mark of man and mathematics, in this case a spool left by the fiber optics people, used now as a garden table. Next, the gentle curve of the retaining wall, nearly smothered, but a line nonetheless. Another wall, a stone wall he and Wifey had built with their hands! And then it was all pillows and marshmallows, clouds and ice cream cones, sagging and drooping. He found himself sneaking peeks, moving very little, as if the shapes were deer or birds that might panic and run from him. Mail box and bird bath, garage and barn and orchard, and the forest beyond, all were meticulously decorated—attended to, ravished.

"Every pine and fir and hemlock wore ermine too dear for an earl," he remembered from some lost literature class, "And the poorest twig on the elm tree was ridged inch-deep with pearl." He was right about the snow, too.

It occured to him that the snow was almost as efficient as darkness at altering things and making them more mysterious. Nothing had escaped; nothing was the same; nothing seemed itself. Everything was now subject to interpretation or mis-interpretation—just the way English teachers like things. His silly pick-up truck looked like a beached whale or maybe a project created by one of those faculty committees with butcher paper. The north side of everything was plastered white; the leeward side was dark, whatever color was there, black or brown or gray—no cranberry or kiwi anywhere. And now, softer, fluffy snow was sifting down, adding the final touches. The wind was gone.

Okay, it was a pretty good snow. Not Minnesota,but good: limiting, but not crippling. The world was transformed,but The Ice Age had not returned: a very sane, well-proportioned snow. And after all those years with one season, it was very satisfying.

Best of all, his preliminary scrutiny of the driveway turned up no trace of Miss Whitby or her stolen grocery cart. She had been dealt with, sublimated, handled, sent back to the past where she belonged. Both she and her mentor had played against a stacked deck and lost. In the unfortunate current vernacular, Game Over.

Mr. Sherman slid the glass door aside and stepped out onto the deck, this time in his $7 deck shoes from WalMart. Immediately, he found himself trying to remember exactly what it was about snow and cold that he especially liked. A puff of wind struck from the open side—the side with the 40-mile view—and the cold and the snow penetrated his fleece ensemble like it was made of doilies.

Okay, not the cold, then: it was not the cold that he had loved. And his ankles now sent a similar message about the snow. Further contemplation would have to happen indoors. After all, he wasn't crazy.

At another window, he examined another view. Sure enough, the snow was a metaphor. Others shovel it; English teachers analyze it. Somewhere down under the snow, things as they used to be were buried, put to rest, settled—at least for the time being. Oh, they were still there, and they were not forgotten, but for now, there was no urgency. The new reality was the snow, and the snow was the present, and the present was powerful. No school today! It would not escape him that his mind had been working like the snow, covering the past, altering its shape, making it something he could do nothing about without spoiling the present. The snow would melt, and growth would follow—dormant things would spring back into life, and forgotten seeds would take root and grow. Stuff like that. An English teacher could go on with that for a long time, and drive himself nuts again. Maybe that's where the term "Snow Job" comes from.

When things are indistinct, you can see what you want, Mr. Sherman decided, and the past is indistinct. He resolved to let it go, make Wifey some coffee, and maybe go out and play in the snow.

He was fine. Really.

BVG